SNOW WHITE & THE HUNTSMAN™

SNOW WHITE & THE HUNTSMAN™

A novel by Lily Blake
Based on the Motion Picture
Screenplay by Evan Daugherty and
John Lee Hancock and Hossein Amini
Screen Story by Evan Daugherty

poppy

Little, Brown and Company
New York   Boston

A note to parents: Please consult www.filmratings.com for information
regarding movie ratings in making viewing choices for children.

Poppy

Hachette Book Group
237 Park Avenue, New York, NY 10017
For more of your favorite series and novels,
visit our website at www.pickapoppy.com

Poppy is an imprint of Little, Brown and Company.
The Poppy name and logo are trademarks of Hachette Book Group, Inc.

The publisher is not responsible for websites (or their content)
that are not owned by the publisher.

First Edition: June 2012

ISBN 978-0-316-21327-1

10 9 8 7 6 5 4 3 2 1

CW

Printed in the United States of America

Who will you be
when faced with the end?

The end of a kingdom,

The end of good men,

Will you run?

Will you hide?

Or will you hunt down evil
with a venomous pride?

Rise to the ashes,

Rise to the winter sky,

Rise to the calling,

Make heard the battle cry.

Let it scream from the mountains

From the forest to the chapel,

Because death is a hungry mouth

And you are the apple.

So who will you be
when faced with the end?

When the vultures are circling

And the shadows descend.

Will you cower?

Or will you fight?

Is your heart made of glass?

Or a pure Snow White?

Once
upon

a time...

It was the coldest winter the kingdom had ever known. Frost covered the gravestones. The rosebushes in the castle garden were nearly bare, their leaves shriveled and brown. King Magnus stood on the edge of the forest with Duke Hammond, waiting for the other army to arrive. The king could see his own breath. The slow, steady clouds expanded in front of his face, then disappeared into the cold morning air. His hands were numb. He didn't feel the weight of the armor on his back, or the way the chain mail pressed against his neck with metal so cold it stung his skin. He didn't worry about the enemies on the other side of the battlefield, and he wasn't afraid.

Inside, he was already dead.

Yet his army stood behind him. One of the horses whinnied through the fog. *It has been nearly a year*, he thought. *She died almost a year ago.* He had held her head in his hands, watched as the life left her eyes. What was he to do?

Who was he without her? He sat in his chambers, his young daughter perched on his knee, but the cloud of grief was too thick. He couldn't hear a word she uttered. "Yes, Snow White," he'd say, his mind somewhere else as she peppered him with questions. "Right, my darling, I know."

Far across the field, he could see the enemy army. They were shadow warriors, a dark clan gathered by some inexplicable, magical force. They stood in the morning mist as ghostly silhouettes—nameless and faceless. Their armor was a dull black. At times it was hard to tell where the forest ended and they began.

Duke Hammond turned to him, his brows knitted together in worry. "From what hell comes this army?" he asked.

King Magnus set his jaw. He shook his head, trying to pull himself out of the stupor that had lingered for months. He had a kingdom to protect, now and always.

"A hell they'll soon revisit!" he yelled. Then he raised his sword, leading his troops to charge.

They raced toward the enemy army, their swords aimed at the figures' throats. Soon the shadows were upon them. The warriors' armor was similar to theirs, but beneath it were black shadows that shifted and swirled like smoke. A faceless warrior ran toward King Magnus, his weapon drawn. The king swung his sword, and the figure shattered like glass, thousands of black shards flying out in every direction. The king looked up, stunned. All around him, his men were attacking the shadows, and one by one, each warrior exploded into the morning mist. The sparkling shards fell to the ground and disappeared into the hard, frost-covered soil. Within minutes, the field was empty. The king's troops stood there, alone, the sounds of their breaths the only thing left hanging in the air. It was as though the enemy army had never been there at all.

The king and Duke Hammond shared a confused look. Through the fog, the king could make out a small wooden structure standing between the trees. He started toward it. When he was twenty feet away, he could see it was a prison wagon. He dismounted his horse and peered inside, noticing a woman cowering in a corner. Wavy blond hair cascaded down her back. A veil hid her face.

She'd been taken captive by the army—who knows what they had done to her? The dark forces were said to have killed and maimed hundreds of prisoners, even some children. He swiftly brought his sword down on the lock, smashing it.

"You are free now. You have nothing to fear from me," he spoke to her, reaching out his hand for the young woman to take. "What is your name, my lady?"

Slowly, the woman turned toward him, her small frame becoming visible in the light. She rested her thin hand in his and lifted her veil. King Magnus stared into the woman's beautiful, heart-shaped face. She had full lips and heavy-lidded blue eyes, and two thin gold braids pulled her hair away from her high cheekbones. She couldn't have been more than twenty years old.

"My name is Ravenna, sire," she said softly.

The king was silent. Everything about her—her nose, her fingers, her lips—was beautiful and delicate. In that moment, he felt the warmth of her hand. He could smell the fresh pine trees around them. He remembered clearly the day he'd met his wife, the only other woman who had ever made him feel this way. It had been summer, with dappled sunlight playing over the leaves of the apple trees.

But in this moment, the sorrow finally lifted. As he stood there before Ravenna, his heart wild in his chest, he suddenly felt alive again.

The king returned to the castle with the young beauty. The seasons changed. That initial joy only grew. King Magnus asked Ravenna to marry him. Each day he fell a little more in love with her, this young woman who had been taken from her home and kept by the enemy army. He was like a teenager in her presence—his cheeks flushed while she told him stories of her life before meeting him, how she'd lived on the edges of the kingdom with her brother, Finn, and her late mother.

The king's daughter, Snow White, would sit beside them at meals, her chin resting in her hands as she studied Ravenna. She was a child still, only seven years old. Together, they were a family. It was what the king had always wanted.

He would watch Ravenna sometimes, how she smiled at Snow White or took her hand and led her around the castle courtyard. She seemed so very happy with them....

*   *   *

When the day of the wedding arrived, Ravenna stood in the back of the cathedral. Through the wooden doors, she could hear the crowd shifting in their seats. Her cheeks were powdered. Her lips were painted a deep blood-red, and her dress was laced up the back so tightly that she could barely breathe. She watched her reflection in the mirror on the wall, the slightest curl on her lips. Tonight, after the ceremony, there'd be no more pretending. She would finally get what she wanted.

"You're so beautiful...." a small voice whispered.

She turned to see Snow White standing in the doorway, watching her. Snow White took the end of Ravenna's long white gown in her hands, pulling it up to keep it off the stone floor. Ravenna beckoned the king's daughter forward with a slight flick of her wrist. "That is kind, child," she cooed. "Especially when it is said that yours is the face of true beauty in this kingdom." Ravenna touched the little girl's cheek. Her skin was as perfect as porcelain. She had huge dark brown eyes and a hint of rose in her cheeks. Whenever she passed handmaids and soldiers alike, they were charmed, dropping down to one knee.

The little girl looked up at her with eyes so innocent, so naive. Ravenna smiled down into the tiny face, knowing that this charade would end soon, and then she would right the wrongs that had been done to her and to her people. "I know it is difficult, child. When I was your age, I, too, lost my mother."

She stroked Snow White's cheek. She could hear the orchestra in the front of the great cathedral starting up. Soon she'd walk down the aisle. It was all coming together as planned.

As she waited for the music to begin, her thoughts drifted back in time to the day the king's men had just arrived in her village. She'd been so young. Ravenna and her brother, Finn, had been in their mother's gypsy wagon. They'd been together always, a small traveling clan, until the day the king's army came. Her mother had held a mirror in front of her face.

"This is all that can save you," her mother told her. Then the older woman took her daughter's wrist and held it over a bowl of white liquid, whispering spells beneath her breath. With a sharp blade, she nicked Ravenna's wrist and let the blood drip into the bowl; the red shone that much more vibrantly against the white. Ravenna drank the potion quickly, swallowing it down. Sometimes, when she closed her eyes, she could still taste the strong, metallic liquid on her tongue. "Drink," her mother had said. "And with it, you will have the ability to steal youth and beauty. For that is your ultimate power and only protection."

The king's men worked their way through each wagon, taking the gypsies out of their homes and killing them. Finn was screaming. He wanted to protect her—that much Ravenna remembered now. Her mother had put her hands on their foreheads and whispered more spells, more words, putting a power in them that connected them both. They would always have each other, and Ravenna would be tied to him until death. Then they were running, so fast Ravenna could barely catch her breath.

They had escaped, but their mother had been left behind. The hair on the back of Ravenna's neck stood up as she recalled the way the soldier pressed the sword against her mother's throat. Her mother had spoken her last words, calling out to Ravenna as she was dragged away. "Be warned," she'd yelled, "by fairest blood it is done, and only by fairest blood can it be undone." Then her mother had fallen to her knees, the gash spilling blood on the grass. Within minutes she was dead.

"Ravenna?" a small voice asked. "Ravenna? It's time."

Ravenna opened her eyes. Snow White was standing behind her, spreading out the train of her dress. The wooden doors had opened. A thousand eyes were upon her, waiting for her to walk down the aisle. She straightened, her blue eyes darkening as they locked on the king. *The little girl is right. It is time.*

That night, as the last wedding guests drank and ate in the castle courtyard, Ravenna took the king to his bedchamber. She lay beside him in her white wedding gown, her long wavy hair loose around her shoulders, watching as he finished his wine. He ran his fingers through her golden hair and finally let them rest on her thin gold crown. Rubies and emeralds dotted the front. The groom was weakened by the day's festivities, his movements slowed from so many drinks. He was an easy target. . . .

She reached under the pillow and pulled out the silver dagger she'd hidden there just hours before. She raised it above her head, focusing on the center of his rib cage, where the bone concealed his heart. In one swift motion, she drove it into his chest, watching his body shudder from the sudden blow. "First I will take your life, my lord," Ravenna whispered as his limbs finally went still. "Then I will take your throne."

She strode out of the chamber and down the hall, leaving the king twisted in the bloody sheets. She moved quickly, descending the stairs to the castle's portcullis. Her brother, Finn, was waiting outside the latticed iron. His army was behind him, the shadow soldiers barely visible in the moonlight. She raised the metal gate, and the soldiers flooded inside. Within minutes, they'd descended on every inch of the castle.

While the soldiers fought, Ravenna returned to her room. She could hear the cries of civilians downstairs, and the clinking of sword against sword as the soldiers locked in battle. One of her brother's men brought in a massive mirror. It looked like a round shield of highly polished bronze. When she was alone, the air outside her room filling with shouts and yells, she gazed into the mirror's reflective surface. It was much bigger than the one her mother had held before her all those years ago, but it held even more magic.

"Mirror, mirror on the wall, who's the fairest of them all?" she asked, leaning toward it.

The surface of the mirror rippled. Liquid spilled onto the floor around Ravenna's feet, re-forming into a bronze statue nearly as tall as she was. The figure appeared as though it was draped in thick fabric, but it reflected back the room around her. The mirror man's face showed Ravenna's face just as it was. "It is you, my Queen," it said. "Yet another kingdom falls to your glory. Is there no end to your power and beauty?"

Hearing the mirror speak, Ravenna knew the magic her mother had given her was boundless. In her presence, kingdoms fell, men perished, and even simple objects took on a magical life, revealing secrets no one else could know. She raised her hands in the air, feeling the fight in her fingertips, remembering all that her family had given up to the king. He was finally dead. The kingdom was hers again. No one could hurt her now, or ever again.

When the fighting ended and the courtyard was silent, she went back down the stairs. The shadow warriors were assembled in the stone courtyard. Blood was spattered on the tables and chairs. Plates were broken on the ground, the remnants of the celebratory dinner strewn everywhere. She didn't shudder at the sight of the bodies, some of them women, slumped over in their seats. The surviving wedding guests and nobles were lined up against the wall, held back by Finn's army.

"What shall we do with these?" one general asked. The women clasped their hands together, begging for mercy. A few noblemen even teared up. They pulled their children close, trying, however uselessly, to protect them. Ravenna shut her eyes and remembered her mother—how *all* the women in her village had been so brutally slaughtered. This was what was meant to happen. It had been the king's mistake—not hers. This was how it was supposed to be.

"To the sword," she said, her voice flat. She wrapped her

robe tight around her and shuddered from the cool night air. Then she turned on her heel to go.

Out of the corner of her eye, she saw Finn holding the little girl. His knife was pressed against Snow White's neck. Something in the girl's face caught her by surprise, this young child who just hours before had held up her wedding dress. Her lips were trembling, and her eyes were brimming with tears.

"Finn—no!" she cried, the words coming out before she could stop them. He narrowed his eyes at her, as if he weren't quite certain who she was. She straightened, trying not to seem weak before her brother, who had just fought so valiantly in her name, never questioning her commands. "Lock her away. One never knows when royal blood will be of value."

Her eyes met Snow White's. The two stared at each other, the chaos swirling around them. Women were dragged outside to be killed. Noblemen struggled against the soldiers' grips. A little boy was screaming for his mother, his face tear-streaked and red. But in that moment, Ravenna saw only Snow White, and Snow White saw only her. Ravenna rested her hand on her chest, wondering what it was that she felt for this young child, the heir to the very kingdom she had overthrown. They were bound together, somehow, by some strange, powerful force.

Ravenna stood there, her hand over her heart, until Finn left for the dungeons, dragging Snow White behind him.

The child's eyes never left hers. She was still glancing over her shoulder, looking back, until she disappeared behind the heavy wooden door.

Part
One

By
fairest
blood

it is

done...

Finn was watching her again. Even lying in her bed, her eyes half closed, Snow White could see his shadow on the dungeon wall. She didn't say anything. Instead, she shook the matted blanket off herself and folded it on the narrow cot. She ran her fingers through her hair, trying to undo the knots that had formed at the nape of her neck. Then she knelt down, starting her fire as she did every day, twisting the wood back and forth, back and forth, until the thin shavings caught. By the time they flared up, bringing warmth to her fingers, Finn was gone.

She held out her hands, taking in the heat. He visited her some mornings, watching her from beyond the bars, his small eyes darting above his long, thin nose. He never said anything, never left anything—not even a plate of food or a jug of water. She wondered if it made him happy to see her now, just past seventeen, still locked away in the tower dungeon. Did he feel any remorse? Did he care? She doubted it. He was his sister's brother.

Snow White pulled her tattered dress around her body, tucking her bare toes underneath the hem. It had been ten winters. At a certain point, she'd stopped counting the days or weeks, instead paying attention only to the changing seasons. She could see the tops of the trees from the cell window. She knew each limb as well as she did her own. In the warmer months, bright green leaves burst from them, spreading out, staying that way through the height of summer. Then they would change. The green gave way to golds and reds, until all of them shriveled and fell, one by one, onto the hard soil.

Now, with the faint traces of spring in the air, she wondered if this year would be different—if it would be the year Ravenna came for her, finally, to end this imprisonment. It had been so long that she almost didn't mind the dank cell anymore. The walls were always cold and moist, smelling of mildew. Light streamed in only once a day, for a little more than an hour, when the sun came over the trees. She always sat there, letting it kiss her face, until it was gone. But the loneliness was what killed her. Sometimes she wanted nothing more than to talk to someone. Instead, she found herself replaying the same memories in her mind, adding new details, changing some, trying to piece together her past.

She thought of her father, how she'd discovered his bloody body the night of the wedding. She remembered the warmth of her mother's hand on her forehead, comforting her before she went to sleep. But more than anything, she always returned to the same moment. It was so vivid, even now, ten years later.

It was right after her mother had fallen ill. The king and Duke Hammond had watched them from the castle balcony, as they did sometimes. The duke's son, William, was her age, and they played together often, chasing each other through the courtyard or rescuing sick magpies. He'd climbed the apple tree, his dark brown hair sticking up in a hundred directions. A toy bow was slung over his back.

Snow White followed him, hugging the tree to keep from falling. When they were fifteen feet up, William plucked an apple from a branch and held it out to her. It was red, without a single mark on it. "Go on," he said, his hand outstretched, waiting for her to take it. He had light brown eyes. When he tilted his face toward the sun, she could see they were speckled with green.

She reached for it, and he pulled it away, biting into it himself. Then he grinned, the *I'm-just-teasing-you* grin she'd grown so accustomed to. "Gotcha!" He laughed. She was so annoyed, she pushed him. He lost his balance, grabbing for her and taking her down with him. They both fell, their breaths knocked out of them when they hit the ground. They lay there panting, until one of them finally laughed. Then they couldn't stop. They'd laughed and laughed, rolling onto their sides. She'd never felt so happy.

Now, years later, she sat in the cold cell, her eyes closed, trying to remember his face. She wondered if he was still alive or if Ravenna's soldiers had tracked him down somewhere beyond the castle walls. The last time she'd seen him was the night of the wedding. In the chaos, Duke Hammond had thrown him onto the back of his horse. One of the duke's bodyguards had put her on another horse, and the four of them raced toward the portcullis, trying to escape. William was yelling to hurry up. The gate was coming down as they galloped toward it. Just when they'd almost made it, an arrow struck the bodyguard in the chest, throwing him from the horse. The horse had reared back, slowing Snow White's escape. William and the duke ducked underneath the portcullis just as it closed, leaving Snow White trapped inside the castle walls.

William screamed for her. She heard him begging his father to go back. But the shadow soldiers were already swarming the courtyard. Her bodyguard writhed on the ground. Snow White was tied up and dragged back into the castle. The last thing she'd seen was William's face as he and his father had galloped away.

The sound of footsteps suddenly echoed down the hall. It was like thunder to Snow White's sensitive ears.

"Let me go!" a girl yelled, her voice barreling through the stone corridor. "Get off me!"

Snow White got up and went to the door. She pressed her face between the rusted bars, trying to get a better look. They rarely kept other prisoners in the north tower. She'd seen only three in the entire ten years she'd been there, and most of them had been awaiting execution. An older man, nearly sixty, had been caught stealing food from one of Ravenna's supply wagons. He was there only a few hours before he was executed. He'd been beaten so badly he could barely speak. The other two prisoners hadn't stayed long, either.

The soldier came down the hall, dragging a young girl in his wake. She couldn't have been much older than Snow White. She had wide-set blue eyes and a pale round face. Frizzy blond hair fell down her back. She strained against the soldier's grasp, but it was no use. He threw her into the cell and closed it, the lock clicking in place.

The soldier started back down the stone corridor, his footsteps growing fainter as he descended the stairs. Snow White waited for silence before she dared to speak.

"Hello . . . ?" she asked. She was surprised by the sound of her own voice. She coughed. "What's your name?" She leaned to the side, trying to get a better view of the girl, who'd disappeared in the back of the cell.

After a few moments, the girl reappeared. She pressed her face against the bars, wiping the tears from her cheeks. "I am Rose," she said softly.

Snow White brushed off her tattered dress. She could only imagine what she looked like, after so many years locked away, with not even a brush to comb out her hair. "How did you get here?" Snow White asked. "Did you commit a crime against Ravenna?"

Rose shook her head. She stared at a spot on the floor, her eyes tearing up. "I didn't do anything," she said. "All the girls in our village were taken. I was trying to reach a safe haven at Duke Hammond's castle when I was caught. I was—"

"The duke?" Snow White said, her voice shaking. "He's alive?"

"Yes," Rose answered. "His village at Carmathan has taken in Ravenna's enemies."

Snow White's throat closed. She'd assumed Ravenna had used her dark magic to find Duke Hammond and William long ago. She'd convinced herself that they were dead. "He still fights in my father's name?" she asked.

Rose studied her up and down, taking in the tangled hair and the dirt that stained her knees. There were holes in the bottom of Snow White's dress. She tried to cover them with her hands. She hadn't even noticed them until now.

"You're...the king's daughter?" the girl asked. *The princess?*" Rose's mouth dropped open. She looked utterly confused.

Snow White nodded. Tears filled her eyes. She thought only of the duke just as she remembered him, sitting at dinner next to her father, laughing a little too loudly at his jokes. He'd lift William up with one great swoop and set him down on his shoulders. She recalled looking up at them, thinking William was the tallest person in the world. She'd always been jealous that he could touch the ceiling.

Rose shook her head. She pressed her finger to her temple. "The night Ravenna's reign began, we were told that all in the castle were put to the sword. How were you spared?"

Snow White shook her head, not wanting to revisit that night. The stink of blood in the stone courtyard. How Finn had taken her up the long, narrow stairway and to the dungeons. Even after all these years, she didn't know why Ravenna had shown her mercy at the last moment.

"William...?" she asked, seeing his face again, those hazel eyes staring back at her through the branches of the apple tree. "The duke's son? Is he still alive?"

Rose gripped the metal bars. "Yes, Princess," she said softly. "He's been fighting for the cause. He's known for surprise attacks on Ravenna's army. I haven't heard about him in a while, but—"

"How long is 'a while'?" Snow White interrupted. William was out there somewhere, beyond the castle walls, fighting still. She was consumed by this new hope. She couldn't help it. The duke and William were like family. Maybe it wasn't too late for her. Maybe Ravenna's army would be defeated yet.

Rose stared at the dank stone floor. "Six months, maybe a little more."

Snow White let out a deep breath. All wasn't lost. There were people still fighting, refusing to give in to the dark forces that had taken her father's kingdom. She caught the tears as they fell from her cheeks.

"Are you all right, Princess?" Rose asked. She leaned over, trying to get a better look.

"I am," Snow White said. She smiled, a small, hopeful laugh escaping her lips. "I've never been happier."

13

R avenna sat on the throne, her generals standing before her. Dozens of candles flickered around the room, warming the cold stone chamber. The Black Knight General in his gleaming black armor dabbed his sweaty forehead with a handkerchief. He still stank from the latest battle—Ravenna could smell him from five feet away.

"There are scattered rebel groups on the fringe of the Dark Forest," he said. Beside him, a general with fiery red hair held up a map of the kingdom. The black knight pointed to the periphery of the Dark Forest. The monstrous expanse of trees was so dangerous that no one ever entered it. "Here and here. But they cause little harm. We have pushed Duke Hammond's forces into the mountains, but his stronghold at Carmathan holds firm."

Ravenna held her head steady, a tall spiked crown perched on her twisted blond braids. She reached toward the bowl on the table beside her. Five dead songbirds lay on their backs, their bellies slit open from beak to tail. She plunged her fingers into one and plucked out its heart. Then she ate the tiny organ—no bigger than a pea—letting the sweet blood trickle down the back of her throat. "Lay siege to it," she said, loving how tender the meat was.

Another general stepped forward from a line in the back. He was shorter than the others, with a thick beard that hung four inches below his chin. "The mountains and forest provide impenetrable protection, my Queen," he said. He wrung his hands together nervously, waiting for her reaction.

Ravenna stood, letting her robe fall back to reveal her full figure in a dress of molten silvery gold. It shimmered as she moved. She appeared as she had ten years before. Her skin was taut and flawless. Not a line marked her face. In fact, she looked even younger than she had when the king had met her, as if each year she became more beautiful. Time could never touch her.

She lurched forward, leveling a finger in the general's face. "Then lure him out! Burn every village that supports him. Poison their wells. If they still resist, put their heads on pikes to decorate the roads!"

The black knight stepped in front of the general, as if trying to shield him. "My Queen," he said, bowing slightly, "*they* have taken the fight to us. Rebels harry our supply lines. Dwarves rob our pay wagons."

Ravenna couldn't take it anymore. Excuses—it was always excuses with these men. She grabbed the pointer from the black knight's hand and rapped him hard across his thighs. "Dwarves?" She smiled, satisfied at the *thwack* sound of wood hitting metal. "They're half men!"

The black knight shook his head. He pulled his metal helmet off, brushing back his greasy brown hair with his fingers. "They were once noble warriors, my Queen." He looked at her, seemingly almost apologetic. "We did capture two rebels. Should we put them to the sword?" he asked.

Ravenna smiled. She reached into the bowl of songbirds and plucked out another heart. She chewed it, enjoying the gentle give of the meat. "No," she said. "I wish to interrogate them myself. Bring them here."

The black knight signaled to a soldier in the back of the throne room. He disappeared out the massive wooden doors. Ravenna paced in front of them, feeling her breath quicken. She hadn't gotten this far to let her kingdom fall to rebels. She would hunt them down, wherever they were. She wouldn't stop until they were all dead, their villages charred and ruined, their children prisoners of the regime. It would take time, but she would do it. She just needed to keep her strength up. Her powers had to remain strong.

She looked out the window to the castle wall below. Peasants crowded around the trash heaps, searching through rotting pig carcasses and moldy tomatoes. A woman with a baby clutched to her chest was yelling. She grabbed a chicken bone from the little boy beside her, wrestling him for it. Ravenna watched them, flicking her metallic shimmery skirts back and forth. She and Finn were once poor

19

like them, gypsies living in a covered wagon. Where had the king been then? He had burned her village. He'd even killed the women, believing them to be traitors. Was she not a more benevolent leader than he?

The soldier returned, dragging two men in his wake. The older one had gray hair and deep lines around his mouth. One of his eyes was bruised and swollen. There was a gash on his arm that was still bleeding. The other was half his age, a handsome young man with broad shoulders and thick muscles that were visible even through his ripped shirt. He appeared untouched.

Ravenna strode forward. They both stared at her defiantly, their eyes ablaze from within. The older one strained against the guard's grip. "Under your rule, we have lost everything," he said, never taking his eyes off Ravenna. "We will not stop until this kingdom is free."

"Not everything," Ravenna said, considering the handsome boy standing right beside him. "Is this not your son? How dare you be so ungrateful to your Queen." She grabbed the boy's face, looking into his stone-gray eyes. Neither of them spoke.

For a moment, the boy let her stroke his cheek. Then, in one swift motion, he pushed the guard, throwing him off balance, reached for the guard's dagger, and drove it into the center of Ravenna's chest.

The room was completely silent. Everyone stared at the dagger. Ravenna nearly laughed. She couldn't feel a thing. The power her mother had given her was so strong, so all-consuming, even the sharpest of swords could not kill her. She pulled the dagger from her chest. The hole closed instantly. There was no blood. There was not even a mark. The skin was completely smooth where the blade had gone in.

The boy looked on in horror. "You would kill your Queen?" Ravenna asked, narrowing her blue eyes at him. She couldn't stop herself. She felt the rage building inside her, the fury. It mixed with her blood, pulsing through her veins, making her feel stronger than she ever had before. "You have beauty and courage. But how strong is your heart?" she hissed in his ear.

She set her hand down on his chest. His face was drawn. He tried to back up, but her magic paralyzed him. She could hear his heart pounding, each beat echoing in her ears, growing louder with each passing second. Somewhere outside her, the boy's father was begging her for mercy. She didn't hear his words. Instead, she let the magic consume her, sweeping her away in its raging current. She leaned back, pouring her strength into her fingertips as his heartbeat sped up. *Faster*, she thought, and his heart pumped faster. *Faster*, she repeated to herself, and the beats sped up even more, one blending into the next, until the sound was so loud she could barely stand it.

The boy's face was frantic. His eyes were bulging and red. She breathed out, using all her strength to close her fist. She could feel his heart in her hand, as if she were inside his chest. She kept closing her fingers, tighter and tighter, until her hand was balled into a fist. He grimaced in pain as she squeezed.

The hammering of his own pulse filled his ears until his heart finally burst. He fell to the ground, dead. His father knelt over him, pounding on his chest, trying to revive him.

Finn raised his sword to strike the old man, but Ravenna stopped him. "No—let him return to the duke and speak of the generosity of his Queen." She nearly laughed as she said it. Then she started out of the throne room, Finn following close behind her.

She could barely walk. He came to her side, helping her with each step. She felt as if all the air had been taken out of her lungs. Her legs were weak, her shoulders stooped forward. She felt the skin on her face. It was now covered with fine lines.

They didn't speak until they reached her chambers. She collapsed in her armchair, her breaths finally slowing.

Finn studied her. "Magic comes at a lofty price," he said finally. Carefully.

Ravenna looked at her hands. There were dark brown spots on the backs of them. The skin was paper-thin. "And the expense grows," she acknowledged. Even those few words drained her.

She knew this by now. Every time she used her powers, it aged her. That was her battle, day after day. But she had to be the all-powerful Queen. She had to be feared and respected across the kingdom, without anyone knowing how quickly her magic waned. There was only one thing that could restore her now.

"Go," she said, her eyes meeting her brother's. "Bring me one. Now."

By the time Finn returned, Ravenna was hunched over, one hand resting on the wall to hold herself up. She didn't dare look in the mirror. She couldn't stand to see what had become of her face. Deep lines were now at the corners of her mouth and her eyes—she could feel them. The skin on her neck hung loose, sagging over her diamond choker.

"I have something for what ails you," Finn said. Ravenna turned, taking in the young girl before her. "What holds more beauty than a rose?" Finn asked.

Rose strained against Finn's grasp. Her skin was a beautiful cream color. She had big, wide-set blue eyes and blond hair. Ravenna smiled, loving everything about this one. She was so young—not even seventeen. She was so . . . *perfect*.

"What are you going to do to me?" the girl asked. She twisted and turned, trying to free herself. Ravenna stepped forward, her footsteps echoing in the massive stone room.

She needed this, more than anything. Not just to restore her youth and energy but also to restore her ability to lead the kingdom. *Yes*, she thought as she brought her hand to the young girl's neck. *The people need their Queen.*

She closed her fingers around the girl's throat. Rose opened her mouth to scream, but no sound came out. Instead, Ravenna could feel the essence of the girl's youth pouring forth, a well of energy just waiting to be tapped. Ravenna leaned back, letting the energy flow out of Rose's mouth and into hers, filling her from her toes up to the top of her head. She felt her skin tighten. The hand that clutched Rose's throat appeared younger now, the age spots gone. Her shoulders were no longer stooped. She stood tall, feeling the power pulsing through her. She would live forever this way, never getting old, always keeping her beauty as it was.

When it was all over, Ravenna released her grasp. Rose dropped to her knees. Her hands were now gnarled. Her face was withered and wrinkled, her hair wiry and gray. She hunched over the floor, her back curved in a C. She looked nearly eighty years old. All traces of the beautiful young girl she had been were gone.

Ravenna stared exultantly at her brother. Even he appeared younger, rejuvenated by Ravenna's new power. The spell their mother used to connect them was more apparent now as Ravenna stared into Finn's face. His skin was radiant, his eyes shining with a new light. He looked even stronger than he had before. His muscles strained against his linen shirt.

She felt no pity for the girl. She felt only power, the sweet drunkenness that came whenever she took someone's youth. There was nothing that could stop her. She was smarter than the smartest men in the kingdom, stronger than the fiercest warriors, and she was more beautiful than all the maidens who had come before her.

She strode into the mirror chamber, wanting nothing more than to see her reflection. The mirror man would confirm what she already knew to be true. She longed to hear his voice again, to be comforted by his magic. "Mirror, mirror, on the wall," she began, "who's the fairest of them all?" She looked into the glossy surface. Her pulse quickened as the mirror melted at her feet and re-formed into the bronze statue. Her own face stared back at her reflection in his smooth, featureless visage.

"My Queen," the mirror said, "you have defied nature and robbed it of its fairest fruit. But on this day, there is one more beautiful than you. She is the reason your powers wane."

Who could be more beautiful than she was? Had she not consumed the youth of some of the most radiant girls in the kingdom? What was it all for? Ravenna balled her hands into fists. There was no one more beautiful than she was, no one more powerful or youthful. The mirror was wrong—it had to be. She rocked with anger. The high she'd felt after conquering Rose was quickly and completely gone. "Who is it?! Give me her name!" she hissed through clenched teeth.

Her reflection stared back at her. "Snow White," the mirror said.

"Snow White?" Ravenna repeated. She swallowed hard. "I should have killed her as a child. She is my undoing?"

The mirror brought its fingers to its chin, stroking it in an attitude of thought. "But...she is also your treasure, my Queen. It was wise that you kept her close. For the innocence and purity that can destroy, can also heal. Hold *her* heart in your hands, and you shall never again need to consume youth. You shall never again weaken or age. Immortality without cost..."

Ravenna stared at her hands, trying to imagine what it would be like to never again see them as she had just minutes before—wrinkled and covered with age spots. What would it be like to never have her breaths shorten, to never feel the weight of the years upon her?

What would it be like to live forever?

She let out a low laugh, the sound of it spurring her on, until she was laughing so hard she was nearly in tears. Snow White. Of course. It had always been Snow White who could bring her this gift. There was a reason she had saved her—she had felt it all these years. There was a reason they were connected. And now it revealed itself to her in all its glory....

"Finn!" she screamed, the laughter consuming her. "Bring me Snow White!"

She kept laughing, the lightness of it comforting her. She pressed her eyes closed, and tears streamed down her cheeks. She would live forever. She just had to kill Snow White and take her heart. It all was so simple, so obvious. How had she not realized it before?

When she finally opened her eyes, she was alone in the chamber. The mirror was just like any other mirror, its reflection revealing the empty room. The mirror man was gone, but his words still echoed in her ears: *Immortality without cost...*

now White pressed her face between the bars. It had been an hour since they'd taken Rose away. Snow White had watched as Finn came upstairs with a soldier and pulled Rose from her cell. She had screamed and kicked, but the soldier had held her legs. They'd carried her downstairs like that, ignoring Snow White as she'd also pleaded for them to stop.

She hoped the young girl was okay. She wanted to believe that it was all a misunderstanding and the girl would go free eventually, that she would not be hurt. But worry consumed her. She knew Ravenna too well. And whatever Rose had done (had she done something?), Snow White could not shake the feeling that today's conversation had been their last.

She wrung her hands together as she paced the length of the small cell. It was hard to wrap her mind around it all. Duke Hammond was alive. William fought in her father's name. The thought of them brought hope. The cell seemed so much smaller now. She couldn't stand the way it smelled of mildew, or how there were always cockroaches scurrying at night. She couldn't take not being in the sun. What had grown dormant after so many years stirred in her again. She needed to be out, away from this dank prison, on the road to find Duke Hammond. She needed her family again.

Almost as soon as the thought crossed her mind, there was a whistling sound. She turned, noticing two magpies perched on the castle ledge. She remembered the distinctive birds from her childhood. Their sleek black feathers made them stand out in the light gray sky. Their tails were more than half the length of their bodies, and their wing feathers were a stunning iridescent blue. They stood there, their heads tilted in her direction, as if she had called them to her by some strange magic.

She went to the window and watched them. They flapped their wings once, the blue feathers catching the light. "Are you trying to tell me something?" she muttered, wondering if she was imagining it. "What are you doing here?" The birds hopped along the ledge to where the tower roof slanted toward the earth. The wood shingles were rotted in places. The black tar was sticky from the sun. It took her a moment to notice the roofing nail sitting directly between the two birds. It stuck out at an angle, just within reach.

Snow White threaded her arm through the metal bars and grabbed the nail. It was three inches long, and the bottom half was still lodged in the wood. She moved it forward, then back, repeating the motion until it felt loose. The birds sat on the roof beside it, watching as she worked at the rusty piece of metal. She'd nearly pulled it out when she heard footsteps down the stone corridor. She heard Rose's muffled cries, then her cell door opening. *She was still alive.* The realization urged her on.

The magpies sensed the danger and flew away, settling in a nearby tree. "Come on," Snow White muttered to herself. She yanked hard on the nail once, then again. Finn slammed the other cell door shut. She heard his footsteps coming closer, approaching her own cell. She yanked one final time, and it came out, sending her falling backward. She scrambled onto her bed and pulled the blanket around her. The rusty nail was still clasped in her hand.

Snow White pretended to sleep. She could hear him just outside the cell. His shoes clacked against the stone floor as he paced back and forth in front of the door. She finally opened her eyes, as if she'd just woken up. "Did I wake you?" he asked. With that, he turned the key in the lock and entered the cell.

Snow White shook her head. She tightened her grip around the nail, wondering what it was he wanted today. "You've never come in before," she said softly. She threaded the nail between her two fingers, letting the rusty tip stick out between them.

Finn tilted his head, studying her. He looked charmed. She offered him a small smile, trying to lure him closer with her eyes. "My Queen won't allow it," he said. "She wants you all to herself."

"I'm afraid of her," Snow White tried. She studied his face. It was exactly the same as it had been the day they met—the night of her father's wedding. His fair skin hadn't aged at all. His nose was pointed at the end, and his blond hair was perfectly cut, combed down in front to cover his large forehead.

He came toward her and rested on the edge of her bed. She counted each one of her breaths, trying to stay calm. She straightened and pulled her legs up toward her, sitting beside him. Her fist was still closed at her side.

"It's all right, Princess," Finn cooed. He reached out and touched her arm. "You will never again be locked in a cell." He was wearing the same black leather suit he always did, the collar coming up to hide his neck. He was so close now, she could see her faint reflection in the polished surface.

Snow White squeezed the rusty nail. "What does she want from me?" she asked, looking up at him. Finn brushed her hair away from her face. His thick fingers stopped on her cheekbone. It took all she had not to cringe visibly at his touch.

Then he reached down for something at his waist. He pulled it from its sheath so quickly, it took her a second to realize what it was. "Your beating heart," he said, tightening his grip on his dagger.

Snow White looked at the glinting blade, then into his unfeeling eyes. She raised her fist. Without any hesitation, she struck him across the face. She held the nail firm, wanting to do as much damage as possible.

A gash opened in his cheek, from the bottom of his left eye to his nose. The blood dripped down his face, spilling over his fingers and onto the wool blanket. "What did you do?" he managed. He tried to get to his feet, but Snow White kicked him hard in the side. She grabbed the keys from his belt and ran for the door, her heart pounding in her chest.

She slammed the metal door behind her to lock it. Then she darted to Rose's cell. Snow White fumbled with the keys, trying the first one on the ring. It didn't work. She tried the next, then the next, but they didn't work, either. She ran her fingers over the remaining keys, her throat going dry. There were nearly forty in all.

"Guards!" Finn yelled down the corridor. "Guards!" His bloody face was visible beyond the bars.

Snow White peered into Rose's cell, horrified by what she saw. Huddled in the back was an old woman, her face shriveled with age. Wiry gray hair fell down her back. She wore the same dress Rose had been wearing earlier and had the same wide-set blue eyes, but she was barely recognizable.

"Go," the old woman urged. She stepped forward and grabbed Snow White's hand. "Just go—please. You'll never make it otherwise."

Snow White gave the woman's hands a final squeeze and released the keys into them. Then she turned to the narrow stairs, which spiraled down to the main castle. She circled down them, taking two at a time, growing more and more dizzy with each flight. She heard Finn yelling somewhere above her even as she descended the last few steps and nearly collapsed on the floor.

The castle's third floor was quiet. She recognized it immediately from her childhood. It was the same wing that Duke Hammond and William had lived in. Each window was covered with deep burgundy drapes, and an ornate wooden wardrobe rested against the far wall. She knew each of these rooms as if they were her own. She started toward the other end of the wing, but just then, two guards ran up the stairs. Their weapons were drawn. She could see it in their eyes—they already knew she had escaped.

"Get her!" one yelled as they ran in her direction.

She escaped back into the stairwell, bolting the door behind her. She didn't bother to look back. They rammed into it, the wood creaking with each violent blow. She had to get to the courtyard. She could raise the portcullis and escape, just as Duke Hammond and William had all those years before. "I just have to make it there," she told herself.

When she reached the bottom of the staircase she burst through the door and into the open air. The light was so bright, it burned her eyes. She shielded her face from the sun. It had been so long since she'd been outside, it was almost too much to take in. Even the wind felt strange against her skin.

Before she could process it, she heard the sound of footsteps behind her. The guards were coming out of the throne room and into the courtyard. There were ten of them, at least. They all wore the same black armor. She looked at the east wing of the castle, where the portcullis was, but two men on horseback were already galloping toward her from their normal posts at the gate. There was nowhere to go.

She froze in place, uncertain about what to do next. As she clutched her hand to her heart, she heard a small whistling sound. The two magpies she'd seen outside her window were there in the courtyard, circling just a few feet above her. She rubbed her eyes, not sure if she was imagining them. They looked so vivid. The sunlight streamed down and caught their blue wings, making them shimmer.

They swooped in front of her, darting toward the west end of the courtyard. The flower bushes there were shriveled and brown. "Just like the nail," she whispered to herself. She followed, knowing that there was something they wanted to show her.

Behind her, the guards were closing in. The two on horseback were nearly upon her. She heard the loud clack of the hooves on the stone.

"Get her! She's trapped!" someone yelled to the pack from the throne room.

She just kept following the two birds. They were approaching the massive stone wall. She looked down, finally realizing what it was they were showing her. There, beneath the wilted shrubs, was the entrance to the castle sewers. It was a hole about two feet across—just wide enough for her to slip through.

As the magpies flew away, she dropped down, sliding across the stone floor on her hip. Then she lowered herself into the sewer system. She hung there for a moment, her fingers gripping the rim of the drain, before letting go. She could barely breathe as she plummeted into the darkness below.

She was instantly swept away by the current of the water. High above her, one guard lowered himself in, trying to follow, but the drain was too small. His hips got stuck. His legs hung in the air above her, kicking frantically.

"Open the gates! The princess has escaped!" one guard yelled above, his voice echoing down the tunnel as she floated away.

Snow White reached out for the wall as she slipped past, but it was coated with slimy algae. The stone was so slippery, she couldn't get a grip. Instead, the thick sludge lodged beneath her fingernails, turning them green.

After so many years locked in the tower, her legs weren't strong enough to keep her afloat. She kicked as hard as she could, struggling against the current, and thrashed her arms. But as the sewage tunnel narrowed, the water pulled her under.

She disappeared beneath the foaming sludge, and the entire world went dark.

The water sucked her into a long, narrow pipe. She could feel the walls closing in on her. Her shoulders brushed past them. She tried to make herself as small as possible, folding her arms over her chest and crossing her legs. She didn't dare struggle—she was too afraid she'd get stuck.

After a few moments, the tunnel ended and she was out in open water, her limbs finally free. Her lungs were throbbing. She desperately wanted to take a breath. She stared up at the surface of the water, nearly twenty feet above her. Seaweed floated by, casting shadows on her face. She kicked wildly, toward the sun, but when she reached the seaweed it was too thick. It tangled around her arms and legs, weighing her down.

This can't be happening, she thought, the reality of her situation sinking in. She kicked frantically, trying to free herself, but a piece of seaweed was still coiled around her leg. She was still so weak. Her lungs hurt. She kept flailing her arms until the surface of the water was inches away. With a few desperate kicks, she finally freed herself and broke through, bursting into the open air.

Gasping for breath, she could hear the distant sound of hooves on the stone. The soldiers were coming for her. She stared at the beach, just a hundred feet away. The castle was nestled into the hillside above the coast. The cliff beside it was covered with trees and shrubs. She swam for the shore, grateful when the waves helped her onto the beach. She didn't have much time.

The shore was covered with large gray rocks. They were assembled in lines, creating a massive maze, stretching the length of the sand. Snow White approached the first stone entrance. It was taller than she was, the walls covered in barnacles and dried seaweed. She went through it, winding into the maze, but when the stone passageway forked in two, she wasn't certain which way to go. Her childhood memory was less distinct when it came to the maze— William had always been the one to find the way out.

Her dress was soaked and she was shaking from the cold. She heard the sound of hooves on rocks. The army was getting closer. Finn had certainly alerted Ravenna already. If he didn't find her, Ravenna's magic certainly would. She would have her heart.

Snow White started to her right. Her hands were shaking. She was about to round a corner when a soft whistling noise caught her attention.

She turned. The two magpies had come back to her. They were sitting on the stone wall to the left. She covered her mouth, tears welling in her eyes. They swooped off the ledge and flew in the opposite direction. She followed after them down the beach, winding in and out of the massive rocks, until the path emptied onto the sand. A few feet in front of her sat a beautiful white mare. It was sitting on the shore, in a way she'd never seen a horse do before, as if it were just waiting for her to climb on.

The sound of hooves came closer. "There!" a man's voice shouted. She looked up the cliff ledge. The first two soldiers on horseback emerged from the trees. One pointed at her with a silver dagger. She didn't hesitate. She ran at the mare, vaulting herself up onto its back. It stood, and they took off down the rocky beach.

They galloped down the shore, the waves crashing beside them. Snow White kept looking back, her hair a mess of black. The salt air coming off the ocean stung her eyes. Finn's army descended the cliff quickly and were still close behind.

Finally, the magpies turned right, back onto the mainland. The mare followed them into the thick forest, and the army pursued Snow White through the trees.

She recognized the land from her childhood. They were just outside one of the villages. She'd sat in parades with her parents, moving through the small towns in their open carriage, waving to the village children. Everyone in the settlement had awaited the royal family. They'd worn their finest clothes and strewn flower petals over the dirt road. But as she

45

approached the village, Snow White hardly recognized it. Most of the houses were burnt piles of rubble. Others were boarded up. The old well in the center of the village was sealed shut.

The mare kept up the pace, flying past the charred schoolhouse. At the end of the dirt path, a few children emerged from a thatched home. There were gaping holes in the roof. Snow White slapped the horse's side, but the animal refused to stop. As the children came closer, she could see why. There was panic in their eyes. They were all so thin, like walking skeletons. One had a bloody nose. Another was so frail, he could barely stand. They moved slowly, staring at the horse with a strange curiosity.

Snow White took off into the forest ahead of her, but as the mare continued on, there were fewer and fewer trees to provide cover. She was exposed, riding through a barren field. Rotting stumps filled a clearing that had once been lush with trees. The grass was scorched black. Everywhere, there was death and destruction. The kingdom was a mere shadow of what it once was.

She kept her eyes on the two birds in front of her as they crested a hill. Beyond the steep incline was a wall of ancient trees, their trunks nearly seven feet wide. Snow White swallowed hard. She'd heard of the Dark Forest as a child. Her mother used to tell her stories of the magic the forest contained—plants that would coil around your legs, strange creatures that haunted the undergrowth, and quicksand that could swallow you whole. No one went into the Dark Forest and came out alive.

Snow White looked back. Finn's army was coming up the hill. Within minutes, they'd be upon her. She urged the mare forward. The horse hesitated, uncertain of the giant trees before them. The forest was surrounded by a dense cloud of fog that oozed out between tree trunks. She couldn't see five feet in front of her. "Come on," Snow White whispered, rubbing the mare's neck.

They started into the forest, the mist encircling them. The magpies had disappeared in the thick white cloud. She glanced up at the tree branches. Strange birds called out from above, their guttural shrieks sending shivers down her back. The mare moved slowly into the forest, just a few steps at a time. Snow White let out a deep breath, her hands shaking. The sounds of Finn's men faded into the background. She could hear only the Dark Forest and all its terrible noises.

The mare took one step forward, then another, and then the ground gave way beneath her. She reared back, sending Snow White tumbling off. Snow White hit the ground hard and gasped to get air back into her lungs. When she looked up, the white mare had disappeared back through the mist.

She lay there for a moment, trying to catch her breath. The ground was soggy beneath her. The thick moss crept over her fingers, as if it were trying to swallow them. A few feet away, she could hear the squishy footsteps as the men made their way through the forest.

She stood and started away from them, unable to see even the ground beneath her feet. The white cloud enveloped her. She looked back and briefly saw the silhouette of a man. She ran faster, trying to get away from Finn's army. She kept going, her breathing ragged and hoarse, until her toe caught under a giant tree root that sent her hurtling through the air. She landed with a thud in a patch of orange and red mushrooms.

A puff of pollen rose up around her. The sticky yellow powder settled on every inch of her body. She knew in an instant that something was terribly wrong. Her head felt light. Her vision blurred. She stood, trying to get away, but the Dark Forest appeared even stranger than it had before. The trees looked like hooded figures, menacing and black, waiting to take her back to the castle. "You shouldn't have left, my dear," one hissed, its branch snaking out to stroke her cheek.

Another hobbled toward her, lifting its giant roots with great effort. "Look what we have here. A princess." It bent forward. Snow White stared into its dark face, the bark marked by an axe.

"Get away from me," she muttered. Her mouth was filled with the sick yellow pollen. She felt it on her tongue. "Leave me alone."

But the forest was closing in. Black bats circled above. She could see their fangs as they flew in front of her. Their mouths were covered with blood.

"Please, no..." she cried as they swooped down, chasing her deeper into the dense wood. "Stay away from me." But she was too dizzy. Her body felt like it was weighed down with stones. She struggled to keep her eyes open as she moved forward, away from Finn's men. But within seconds, she fell, the magic pollen sending her into a strange, heavy sleep.

Ravenna circled the mirror chamber over and over, dragging her fingernails against the stone walls. Her chain gauntlet bracelets rattled. The skin around her nails was pink and bloody, but she didn't care. She could think only of Snow White. The girl was off somewhere, outside the castle walls, her heart still beating inside her chest. She was still alive.

Ravenna had lost her chance. So many years locked up in that tower, but now Snow White was gone. Ravenna wondered why she had not seen it before. Those bloodred lips, that flawless fair skin. Hair black as night. Her natural beauty had always been there, just waiting to be consumed. But now it was too late.

There was a faint knock. The door opened, and Finn peered inside, his face raw from where Snow White had slashed him. Ravenna turned on him in a rage and swirled around to attack, her fists landing hard against his chest.

"You swore to protect me!" she yelled, each word filled with pain. "Do you not understand what the girl means to us? This is my future. This is my *everything.*"

Ravenna could barely breathe. She felt the walls closing in on her. She would be stuck like this forever, her powers vulnerable, as long as Snow White was free.

"I told you," Finn spoke quietly, as if nothing were amiss, cupping her hands in his own. "She was chased into the Dark Forest. She's probably already dead."

Ravenna shook her head. It was Finn's fault—her own brother! He had done this to her. There was no loyalty even inside the castle walls. There was no one she could trust. This girl, so young, so fragile, had escaped using only a nail.

Had he *let* her go? Had he given up too easily, knowing that his failure would mean her freedom? He had spent so many mornings up there, studying her, watching her sleep. *I knew it*, Ravenna thought, her grip tightening around his hands. *Somewhere inside him, he loves her.*

"She's no good to me there, lost," she growled. "I have no powers in the Dark Forest. I must have her heart." She landed her fist on his chest once more, satisfied when he winced in pain.

She went to hit him again, but he grabbed her hand. "Have I not given everything to you?" he asked. His gray eyes stared at her, as if to remind her of all the orders he'd carried out in the past—the citizens he'd imprisoned and murdered, and all the young girls he'd brought to the castle for her consumption.

Ravenna pulled her hand away. "Have *I* not given everything to *you*?" she hissed, reminding him of their bond. "*Everything?*" She stayed strong and powerful for him. Without her magic, the opposition would've already taken the castle. They would have both been killed.

They stayed like that for a moment, glaring at each other, until she reached out and touched his cheek. She ran her thumb over the open wound. It closed beneath her touch, the blood disappearing, the skin healing with her magic. When she removed her hand from Finn's face, it was just as it had been before. His skin was taut. There were no wrinkles. There wasn't even a scar.

He ran his fingers over the place where the wound had been. "I won't fail you again," he whispered, bowing his head in reverence. "I have brought you someone who knows the Dark Forest well. A man who can hunt her, should she have survived."

For the first time all afternoon, Ravenna's agitated pulse slowed. She looked at Finn, who was smirking, as if he'd known this all along.

"Good, my brother." She smiled. A dark laugh spilled from her lips. She laughed again, much harder the second time, imagining Snow White out there alone. They would simply retrieve her. Within one day's time, she'd be back. "Very good, Finn," she said, taking her brother's arm and starting toward the door. "Now bring me to him...."

Eric walked to the throne room window, watching the ravens outside. They perched on the stone ledge, their backs hunched, staring at the hillside below. They were wretched things. He remembered them from the day Sara was buried. They'd sat on the roof of the church, their heads tilted, always watching. Two uninvited guests. The whole ceremony, they'd stayed there, darkness incarnate, cawing every now and then. When the priest had gone back inside, Eric couldn't stand it any longer. He'd thrown rocks at them, cursing himself when he'd missed.

Now, years later, he was standing in the Queen's castle, his shirt soaked with whiskey. His pants were filthy, his pockets empty. He was just as angry and sad as he had been then. Sara—*his* beautiful Sara—was gone. He slapped his hand against the glass, scaring away the ravens.

Across the room, two soldiers raised their swords, threatening him. He laughed them off. His entire body hurt from the night before. There was a sharp pain in his right temple whenever he moved his head. If he turned quickly, the room began to spin. The effects of the alcohol had yet to wear off. "So, where is she?" Eric called out to the two soldiers by the door. His voice echoed in the massive throne room. Neither of the men in black armor answered.

He'd been drinking at the village tavern, drunker than he'd been in days, when he was summoned here. It hadn't been his choice, really. When they'd thrown him over the back of a horse, he'd simply been too inebriated to resist. "The Queen demands your presence," the man had said. That much he remembered. But Eric still didn't know why. He was feeling utterly useless these days. There were cows that were more productive than he was. If the Queen needed someone's help, it couldn't be his. He ran his hand through his greasy hair to slick it off his face.

The Queen strode into the room, a young man right behind her. Eric hardly noticed him; his vision was too fixed on the woman's beauty. She was radiant. Her skin glowed, her cheeks pink, her blond hair braided away from her face. She opened her jet-black robe to reveal an off-the-shoulder gown, her bosom bursting from the top of her dress. The metallic fabric was studded with wolves' teeth. She stared at him with her piercing blue eyes. Her gaze demanded he stand up straight. He did at once. Technically, she was his Queen. The *dark* Queen. He'd never seen her so close before.

She walked toward him until they were just inches apart. The silver crown was perched on her head, the decorative looped chains hanging down her sides. She caught a whiff of his sweaty shirt and scrunched her nose.

"My brother tells me you are a widower, a drunkard, and one of the few who have ventured into the Dark Forest." She gestured to the man in a leather jacket standing behind her. Eric realized the Queen's brother was the same man who'd found him at the tavern and brought him here. "One of my prisoners has escaped there," she went on.

Eric shook his head. "Then he's dead—"

"*She*," the Queen corrected, holding up a jeweled finger.

Eric crossed his arms over his chest, trying to steady himself. The room seemed like it was moving. "Then *she* is *certainly* dead," he corrected.

The Queen leaned in so close that the chains of her headdress brushed his leather tunic. Her perfume smelled of dead roses. "Find her. Bring her to me."

Eric shook his head. He had been a Huntsman years ago, before Sara died. He had tracked prey to those woods and nearly lost his life. Even with the best weapons and maps, most people never got more than a quarter mile inside the trees. "I've been to the Dark Forest enough times to know I'm not going back," he said.

He turned to leave, but the Queen clamped down on his arm. "You will be rewarded handsomely," she purred.

Eric laughed. As if that mattered. "Coin's no good to me if I'm lying dead with crows picking out my eyes."

But the Queen did not let go of his arm. Instead, she tightened her grip on him, her nails digging into his skin. She smiled, then leaned in, her lips just inches away from his. "You *will* do this for me, Huntsman."

Eric looked at her hand on his arm. So it wasn't a request—it was an order. "And if I refuse?" he asked.

The Queen nodded to the men by the door. They lowered their lances and aimed the spiked tips at him. Eric stared at the glinting blades and felt nothing. No fear. No sadness. She was threatening his life, but she had pegged him wrong. She couldn't take something he no longer wanted.

"Do me the favor," he scoffed, holding out his arms and closing his eyes. Sara's face came back to him. She was screaming, the bloodstain spreading out on her dress, surrounding the mark where the intruder had stabbed her. "I beg you," he added.

When he opened his eyes, the Queen was still watching him. "So you wish to be reunited with your beloved?" she asked. He staggered back a step, wondering how she knew about Sara. What was the extent of the Queen's power? Had she read his thoughts?

His chest filled with rage. Hearing those words—*your beloved*—spoken from this witch's mouth was too much. What did she know about his beloved? He grabbed the Queen's throat. Her bracelets rattled. "My wife is none of *your* concern," he growled.

The soldiers rushed forward, but the Queen held up her hand, telling them to step back. Her eyes were watery, her face red from the trapped air inside her lungs. She kept looking at him, though, a strange smile on her face, as if she enjoyed toying with him. He released her, wanting to be as far from her as possible. He stepped to the side, but she stepped in front of him, not letting him leave.

"You miss her?" she wheezed. She rubbed her throat where he'd grabbed her. "What would you give to bring her back?"

Eric didn't answer. He could feel the hard knot rising in the back of his throat. Those nights when Sara visited him were the hardest. He would see her face in a dream. He'd kiss the tiny mole on the side of her neck or press his nose into her hair, smelling that sweet mixture of soap and gardenia oil. She was so vivid then, even more so than she'd been in life. He'd wake up heaving, his face swollen and wet, wishing she'd come back to him.

He wiped at his eyes, trying to avoid the Queen's gaze. "Surely you have heard of my powers," the Queen continued. "Bring me the girl, and I will bring back your wife."

"Nothing will bring her back," Eric said loudly. He had buried Sara in a grave at the edge of the village, laying her body in the cold earth. He'd set the tombstone himself.

The Queen brought her hand to his chin and waited until he met her gaze. She was staring so intently at him, her face serious. "*I* can," she snarled. "Believe me, Huntsman. A life for a life."

There was something in that look. Those blue-gray eyes stared right through him, as if she could see everything past and present—all the fear and hurt he'd encountered. The things he wished most for in the world. She knew his life, his soul, how he spent mornings in the dark tavern, drinking to forget. She knew that no matter how hard he tried, Sara always returned to him in his thoughts. He found himself still speaking to her, singing the songs she sang. He saw glimpses of her in the passing faces of strangers.

Who was this prisoner—this stranger—to him? What did it matter if the Dark Forest was his end? Slowly, surely, he met the Queen's eyes and nodded. So it would be done. He would go there, forge his way through those haunted woods, and retrieve the prisoner.

He had nothing left to lose.

ric stood at the entrance of the Dark Forest, watching the shadows lurking between the trees. He'd been there before, but he'd never made it more than a hundred feet in. His last visit had been after the Queen had come to power. Food was scarce. He tracked a young buck across the clearing when it darted into the swirling mist. Everyone in the village knew that the Dark Forest swallowed men whole. Everyone knew of the giant snakes that coiled around your leg, slowly squeezing the life from your body, and the poisonous flowers that could kill with one touch. But his stomach was empty, and it was hard to resist a week's worth of meat.

Within minutes of entering the mist, he was bitten by a spider. It was a giant red-and-gray thing that had dropped down from one of the trees. He hadn't even noticed it until it was upon him. It took him three weeks to recover. The flesh rotted around the bite. He had a fever for nearly a week, which grew worse as it wore on, the violent convulsions waking him in the night. He'd sworn he would never come back.

But now, after suffering through his own hell, the Dark Forest didn't seem as threatening. He was alone. He had no one waiting for him back at the tavern. Everything the Dark Forest could take from him, he had already lost.

"Do exactly as I do," he said to Finn, who was standing behind him with four of his soldiers in tow. They were all sweating profusely, their faces pale with fear.

Eric started into the mist. His hands were shaking from so many hours without a drink. He reached for the flagon of grog at his side but then stopped, thinking better of it. He could celebrate once they found the prisoner.

They walked briefly past some trees before the ground turned into wetlands. He stepped into the bog, pressing his boot onto one of the mossy stones in front of him. It sank down an inch into the wet marsh, but the stone was firm enough to hold his weight. He stepped onto another stone, then another, listening to the quiet sloshing of the mud beneath him. The dirt held poison in it—he could tell by the bones of small animals sticking out of its depths. Finn followed behind him, and his men came after. They kept on like that in silence, taking the giant marshland one stone at a time.

Eric made it across first and turned to help the others gain firmer ground. Giant birds circled high above. One swooped down, just missing a soldier's head. Eric listened through the woods for snapping branches or rustling leaves. He heard only the strange whispers of the forest. People said the woods preyed on your weaknesses and the dark forces could call to you, knowing your deepest desires. As he stalked forward, the words were inaudible, but he could hear faint voices coming through the trees.

Finn moved past him, starting into a field of mushrooms, but Eric grabbed his arm. "*Exactly* as I do," he said. Then he pulled his sweaty shirt up out of his leather vest to cover his nose and mouth. Finn and his men did the same.

As they walked through the mushroom field, pollen flew up around them, some yellow bits sticking to their faces and hair. Eric knelt down, studying the smashed mushrooms at his feet. There was a whole line of them. They led out of the field and into a patch of thin trees. He moved a few mushrooms aside, revealing a stray footprint in the dirt.

He kept his eyes on the trees in front of him. Something moved behind them. He was so focused, he didn't notice that one of Finn's men had wandered to the other edge of the field, where a pool spread out, its surface reflecting the gray sky. Eric turned just as a shadowy creature emerged from its depths, spearing the man through his chest with its barbed tail. Within seconds, the man was dragged under, his back disappearing beneath the glassy surface.

The other men turned to run, but Eric held up his hand to stop them. He pointed to the thin gray trees. He was certain the escaped prisoner was in there—he could hear her struggling against the tangled undergrowth. Eric was about to draw his axe when a branch snapped. A figure emerged from the trees and ran in the opposite direction, farther into the Dark Forest.

Eric gave chase, letting his shirt fall from his face. He moved quickly through the thick fog, trying not to plant his feet anywhere for too long, scared that the moss and vines would twist themselves around his ankles. His prey was just twenty feet off. She moved through the dense woods, weaving in and out of the trees, until she disappeared into the fog. Eric slowed down, searching the misty terrain. He spotted some thick bushes up ahead, just to his right. The branches were broken where she had gone in.

In one swift motion, he reached into the shrub, his hands clasping one of her legs. It didn't take much strength to drag her out, but she fought him anyway, writhing under his grip. She was a small thing.

"Let me go!" she screamed. She turned over, her giant brown eyes staring up at him.

He stepped back for a moment, uncertain what to do. She was so much younger than he'd imagined—no more than seventeen. Her legs were covered with scrapes and bruises. She had the whitest skin he'd ever seen, with full red lips and black hair that fell down her back. When he'd heard of the prisoner, he'd imagined a vicious old hag wielding knives or something. This girl—this *beauty*—he definitely wasn't expecting.

He helped her up, keeping his hand tight around her arm. She struggled back, sinking her heels into the dirt.

When he wouldn't let go, she bit into his hand, drawing blood.

"Enough!" He pulled her back toward the clearing, trying to bring her where Finn and his men were waiting.

But the girl struggled against him, landing a hard blow into his neck. "She's going to kill me!" she screamed. Tears filled her eyes. "I was her prisoner for ten years, and now she's going to kill me for no reason. I haven't done anything wrong."

Taking in her tattered dress and knotted hair, Eric thought she was probably telling the truth. Ten years, though… *Why would the Queen need to lock up a little girl?*

Eric shook his head, trying not to give in to the girl's desperate pleas. "It's not my business what you did. But you aren't the first prisoner to claim they were innocent."

The girl's legs gave out beneath her. She dropped to the ground, turning to dead weight. "Please—you have to believe me," she said, straining against his grasp. "Her brother tried to cut out my heart."

Eric looked down at her. She was shaking. Tears rolled down her cheeks. She kept staring at him with those huge brown eyes. He'd never seen someone so terrified in his entire life.

"I swear it," she said.

Eric looked back through the Dark Forest. He wanted a moment to think. He wanted somewhere to sit, have a swig of the grog, and think the whole thing over. But Finn and his men were coming toward him, their thin shirts still covering their faces.

"Quick work!" Finn yelled. He pulled down his collar and wiped the pollen from his eyes.

Eric studied him. He'd never liked his thin, weasel-like face or the nose that pointed at the end. The girl stood and hid behind him, trying to get as far away from Finn as possible.

"Him," she whispered. "He's the one who came at me with a knife." Her hands shook violently as Finn neared.

"What do you intend to do with her?" Eric asked, stepping forward to slow Finn down.

Finn's top lip curled in displeasure. "What do you care, Huntsman?" He turned to the three remaining guards, signaling for them to move in.

Eric tightened his grip on the girl. His head was throbbing from so many hours without a drink. Sweat beaded on his forehead, but he still felt drawn to fight. "I'll keep my word when the Queen keeps hers," he said. He loosened his grip on the girl's arm, now stepping back, pushing her deeper into the forest and away from Finn's men.

Finn wiped his sweaty bangs out of his eyes. "You *are* a drunk and a fool," he laughed. "My Queen has many powers; she can take life or sustain it. But she can't bring your wife back from the dead."

Eric winced, the words stinging in ways he didn't know possible. "But she told me…" he said. He realized he had been foolish enough to allow a tiny shred of hope to creep back into his heart.

When he closed his eyes, he could still see Sara as he'd found her that day. She had worn her favorite dress—the one with the tiny lilies embroidered on the collar. The knife had gone into her side, just below her rib cage, tearing apart the fabric. Another gash was across her neck. The villagers said someone had come to pilfer supplies—the two gold coins Eric had, the jarred fruits and vegetables hidden below the washbasin. Sara had tried to stop them. By the time Eric had gotten there, her hands were stiff and cold.

Reliving the anguish, Eric couldn't stop himself from crying out, "I want her back!" It was a cry of pure pain.

The Huntsman suddenly knew what he needed to do.

He pushed the girl back farther, trying to get her away from the men. As soon as she was out of reach, she ran into the trees, not bothering to look back. Eric pulled the knife from his waist. He flicked his wrist, throwing it into one guard's chest, right beside his heart. The man fell to the side, grabbing a tree for support. Then Eric drew the two hatchets he carried on his belt. He wielded them in the air—one in each hand.

Finn stalked forward. He held his sword at an angle, waiting to get close enough to Eric's neck. The other two guards rushed in first. Eric knocked one in the head with the blunt end of one of the hatchets. The guard stumbled back, momentarily stunned. He touched his hand to his blond hair, where a wound had opened. Eric swiped at the other, but the guard lunged to the side. Eric continued to fight the man, blocking each blow as it came. But then, out of the corner of his eye, he saw Finn raising his sword. Finn was moving in, ready to strike.

Eric hurled a hatchet into Finn's chest. Finn staggered to the side. The other two guards backed up, eyeing the remaining hatchet in Eric's hands. For a moment, no one moved. They all watched as Finn regained his footing. As if by magic, there was no blood around the wound. His face returned to normal—a sneer was the only sign that he'd been hit. He pulled the hatchet out of his chest and laughed, feeling the smooth skin where it had entered. His shirt was ripped, but he was otherwise fine.

"The Queen has given me protection," he said darkly. "Her touch has transferred power—I cannot be wounded. Not here, inside the Dark Forest." He laughed as he threw the hatchet at Eric. It missed, the blade lodging in a nearby tree trunk.

Eric's throat went dry. He'd never seen anything like it before—a man who could not be wounded. If anything, he looked strengthened by the blow. Finn was glaring at him, the veins in his neck visible as he raised his sword.

Eric tried to block him, but his arm didn't come up in time. Finn's sword pierced him in the side. The metal burned as it ripped through his flesh. He twisted away, hoping it hadn't gone in too deep. When Finn pulled it out, blood spilled from the wound, trickling down Eric's side and onto his tattered gray pants.

The guards stepped back, as if to let Finn finish him off. Finn lunged, but Eric dodged the final blow, instead taking Finn out at the ankles with his right foot. Finn hit the ground hard. He lay there for a second, momentarily stunned.

Eric leaned down. He grabbed Finn by the back of his shirt and picked him up, wincing at the pain in his side. Then he flipped him into a stray patch of mushrooms, watching as a yellow cloud expanded above him. Eric covered his nose, careful not to breathe in any of the pollen.

The other two guards brought their shirts over their mouths. Finn tried to stand, but the pollen had already taken hold of him. His eyes glazed over. He stumbled forward, his hands outstretched, feeling around for something the rest of them couldn't see. He was smiling now, the yellow dust covering his hands. A clump of it was stuck to his chin.

Eric touched the wound in his side, looking at the blood on his fingers. He eyed the guards just a few feet away. They were standing between the trees. They had their swords out, the silver blades aimed at his throat. He couldn't take both of them—not now. Not wounded like this.

Eric glanced over his shoulder at the Dark Forest. The mist had thinned out. The strange voices whispered to him. For the first time, he swore he could understand the words. They were calling from the darkness, urging him to go. He yanked his hatchet from the tree and turned, running as fast as he could into the dense undergrowth after the girl.

Snow White darted through the woods. She kept her eyes on the ground, jumping over fallen trees and winding around stray mushroom patches, careful not to kick up the dangerous pollen. Prickly bushes cut her legs. A branch whipped her arm, raising a hard, pink welt. Still, she kept moving, too scared to even look back.

She cut through a field of red flowers. The dirt squelched beneath her feet, threatening to pull her into the mud forever. She kept going, yanking one foot out, then the other, until she was across. She started down a hilly incline to where a long stream opened beyond the mist.

So they had found her here. They had come into the Dark Forest, risking death to retrieve her. And they'd brought that awful man, his clothes stained with sweat and grog. She'd never seen someone so foul. Who was he? And why had he agreed to go into the Dark Forest for the Queen?

She could understand why Finn would follow her. Ravenna controlled him, telling him what to do, what to say, how to be. The choice was never his to make. The guards simply did what they were told.

But the Huntsman—that's what they'd called him, hadn't they? Why would he come in here, risking his life, if he didn't need to? They'd mentioned something about his wife—that much Snow White remembered. His face had gone pale when Finn had said her name out loud. *Is she being kept prisoner? Is that the Queen's hold over him?*

Snow White continued down the steep incline. The thin vines that clung to the side of the hill slithered forward and wrapped around her ankles, tethering her to the earth. She ripped them off as she moved closer to the black stream. When she'd almost reached it, a heavy hand came down on her shoulder. Another covered her mouth, preventing her from screaming. The reeking Huntsman pulled her to him, one finger over his lips to signal quiet. When he didn't hear anything after a moment, he released her, his face breaking into a relieved smile.

She was filled with loathing. He had tried to give her to Finn. He was working with Ravenna's soldiers, ready to hand her to them so they could cut out her heart. But now what? She was aware that he had *let* her go—that she would be dead already if he wanted her to be. Why the change? And why was he still following her? The uncertainty filled her with rage.

She wheeled her fist back and then punched him as

hard as she could in the mouth. He stumbled backward. As she pushed past him, he put his fingers to his mouth, feeling the blood on his lip.

"Run," he barked before she was a few feet down the muddy bank. "You won't make it a hundred yards, but the warning has been made, so my conscience is clear." He shrugged.

This Huntsman was profoundly irritating. She paused anyway, though, looking closely at the stream. It was filled with eels. Their dark bodies twisted beneath the surface. There were so many, they'd turned the water black. She swallowed hard, feeling that maybe—just maybe—he had a point.

She stared into the water, afraid to go any farther. They were both quiet for a moment.

"Why does the Queen want you dead?" he asked. She turned, for the first time noticing his gray eyes. He had thick, muscular arms and a broad chest. His straw-blond hair came down to his shoulders. She looked at his side, realizing he'd been slashed in the scuffle. Blood stained his shirt, spreading below his leather vest.

"You're hurt," she muttered, watching him press his hand to his side. He nodded, still waiting for her reply. Snow White looked at the ground. "She takes from all the young women in the kingdom. She steals their youth and beauty.... I've seen what happens to them."

"You escaped, though," the Huntsman said. "How long were you there?"

Snow White scanned the Dark Forest, making sure there were no figures lurking in the mist. "I spent ten years in the north tower."

"*Who are you?*" he whispered in vexation. He scanned her ripped clothes and tangled hair again.

Snow White wiped the sweat from her forehead, realizing how she must look. Her velvet bodice was worn and threadbare in spots, the shift underneath stained and torn.

"Who are you?" he asked again, much louder this time.

She glanced around. They were in the middle of the Dark Forest. She had no idea which trail led back to the village, or whether she could even find it. High above, the trees moved, their branches bending unnaturally low, as if they were reaching for her. This man—this *Huntsman*—was her only chance. "I'm the daughter of King Magnus," she finally said.

The Huntsman shook his head. He looked unconvinced. "The king's daughter is dead. She died the same night as her father."

She stared at him, defiant, daring him to question her again. He pressed his fingers to his chin and circled her. "I don't believe it," he muttered under his breath. He peered closer at her jet-black hair, the milk-white skin that hadn't seen sun since she was a child. Snow White stood up straight, letting him notice the big brown eyes she had shared with her father and the soft red lips.

He stopped in front of her, his head down. He gently took her hand and lifted it, turning her arm over to look at the scrapes and bruises marring her skin. She held her breath, unsure how to react. He must have been holding his breath, too, for he suddenly exhaled.

Then he firmly gripped her arm and started off, dragging her along as he trudged beside the muddy stream.

"Where are we going?" she yelled, dismayed by his abrupt violence.

"It's not safe here anymore," he said. "Especially for the king's daughter. They're not going to let you go easily. They might just be stupid enough to follow us deeper into the forest."

She couldn't argue with that. But she shook her arm out of his grasp and trudged along without his help.

They walked for what seemed like ages. Snow White listened to his steady footsteps as the light in the forest dimmed. The darkness between the trees seemed even more menacing now. Shadows darted through the bushes beside them. Snow White tried to ignore them, instead moving faster over rocks and fallen trees, but she could hear the wild animals breathing in the dark.

While they moved, the Huntsman spoke briefly. He told her his name. He'd been summoned by the Queen to lead the small group into the Dark Forest—a place he'd gone into before while tracking animals.

When Snow White asked about his reward, he'd said only that she had lied. He didn't mention his wife, or what the Queen had promised him. She'd wanted to ask more, but his eyes had welled up at the mention of it. Then he'd turned away, trudging up ahead, out of earshot.

They followed the stream for another hour and then started up the incline, where the forest opened up to a small clearing. The dirt was mostly free of vines and plants, making it seem like one of the safer places to rest. Snow White sat on a rotted log. Eric lowered himself down beside her. He unbuckled his belt and peeled his vest and shirt off, exposing the wound in his side. She winced just looking at it.

He moved slowly, trying to get to the flagon of grog.

"Here," she finally said. "Let me help you." She unscrewed the heavy canteen, holding it out to him.

"Can you pour it on?" he asked. He nodded down at the two-inch gash where the sword had gone in. "I don't think it hit anything vital. I wouldn't have gotten this far otherwise."

Snow White doused the wound, cringing as he twisted, obviously in pain. Then she ripped at the hem of her linen dress, working until she got a square piece—the cleanest she could find. She pressed it against his side. "You're welcome," she finally whispered when Eric was silent for a long while.

"We'll stay here for the night," he said.

Snow White cleared a space on the ground and sat down. She looked at him. He was still clutching the tattered rag to his wound. He scanned the trees over her shoulder.

"You never answered me," Snow White said.

"I don't recall a question." Eric brushed the sweaty hair off his forehead.

Snow White curled into a tight ball, trying to steel herself against the cold. "Where are we going?" she repeated.

Eric leaned forward. The tree roots around them glowed with an eerie phosphorescent light, giving them just enough to see by. He grabbed a stick from the ground and drew a box, a few triangles, and a giant circle. He pointed to the box. "Here's the Queen's castle," he said. Then he moved the stick, pointing to the triangles and circle beside it. "The mountains and the Dark Forest. Here, past them—there's a village."

Snow White shook her head. She took the stick from him, writing the words in the dirt: DUKE HAMMOND. She underlined his name twice. "I need to go to the duke's castle."

Eric grabbed the stick from her hand. "You'll go where I take you."

She studied the Huntsman's clothes, noticing his weathered boots and the pants that were worn through with holes. If he wouldn't do it out of sheer goodness, surely there were other reasons for him to do it. "There's a reward that awaits you," she offered. "There are noblemen there—an army."

Eric pulled his shirt back on, seemingly oblivious to the dried bloodstain that spread out on the side of it. He laughed. "The duke fights? He hides behind walls. I know sheep that have more fight than him."

"They'll give you two hundred gold pieces," Snow White continued, undeterred. "Do we have a deal?"

The Huntsman took a giant swig from his flagon. He wiped his lips with the back of his hand and then smiled. "Fine. I'll deliver you to safety, m'lady."

Snow White leaned in close, searching his eyes. She could smell the alcohol on his breath. "Swear it."

"I swear," Eric said. "Constantly. It's one of my better qualities." He smirked, a dimple appearing in his cheek.

She glared at him, ignoring his attempt at charm. He would either do it or he wouldn't—there was no time for games. Finally, he nodded, his smile gone, as if to show he was sincere. "It's a deal, then," she said.

She went to the edge of the clearing and grabbed an armful of dried leaves. She laid them over the dirt, then another armful, trying to create some semblance of comfort. Then she lay down on the makeshift cushion, scattering more leaves over herself. She stared at the black forest above. Giant birds cut across the sky. A low growling sound could be heard in the distance. She pulled her tattered dress around her, trying to warm herself. Tomorrow they'd start off again, on their way to Duke Hammond's. With a little luck, she could reach the stronghold within a week.

She turned to Eric, who had lain down beside the old log, his hand clutching the bloody gauze. "Do you think . . . ?" she said, the worry returning now that the night was upon them. "Will they follow us?"

Eric turned to her, his eyes lit up by the glowing tree roots. "I don't know. They'd be foolish to—few survive." He scratched his head, then took another swig of his drink.

"Is that good news or bad?" Snow White let out an uncomfortable laugh. Eric didn't answer. Instead, he just shook his flagon, trying to determine how much grog there was left. She sat up and studied the Huntsman's face, wondering about this guide she'd just hired. "How far have you traveled into the Dark Forest?"

"We passed it a few miles back," he mumbled. She pulled more leaves around her, searching the woods, but he didn't seem to notice. He just kept sipping that stupid flagon. He took one sip, then another, not stopping until his movements slowed. His eyes fell shut. Within minutes, he was snoring happily, leaving Snow White all alone.

The terrible noises of the forest surrounded her. Every snapping branch or crying bird sent chills through her entire body. She closed her eyes, willing the rest of the world away, but she felt insects crawling up her legs. Something buzzed in her ear.

It was a long time before she could sleep.

The Huntsman hacked through the thick under-growth with his two axes, cutting down the vines and stray branches that blocked their passage. Snow White followed a few feet behind him, lis-tening to the strange voices that whispered through the trees.

"What is that?" she asked. She couldn't make out the words, but they kept calling to her, relentless.

"Pay them no mind," Eric said. He swiped at some thornbushes with his axe. "The Dark Forest gains its strength from your weakness."

The Huntsman continued on. Snow White started after him, but the path closed behind his back. A thornbush caught the side of her dress. She grabbed the soft fabric and pulled, but the branch wouldn't let her go. Instead, it seemed like it held tighter, the barbs twisting in the thick linen. When she looked up, she could barely see Eric in front of her. Vines snaked out from the trees, the grass rose up around her feet, and the tree limbs leaned in, coming just inches from her face.

"Huntsman!" she yelled. She pushed the branches back, trying to step through, but it was no use. The forest was swallowing her whole.

The more she struggled, the more the vines grew in thick coils around her. Leaves spread out in every direction, blocking her view. It was getting hard to breathe. She tried to raise her foot, but a branch had grown over her toe. She strained against it until it snapped. "Huntsman!"

Then, finally, she heard footsteps in front of her— somewhere beyond the tangled wall of green. An axe came down just inches from her right arm, cutting the vines that reached for her. He slashed at the forest to her left and above her, the broken limbs and leaves falling around her feet in heavy piles. She stepped forward, but her dress was still caught, that one thick, thorny branch refusing to let it go.

The Huntsman pulled a smaller knife from his belt. He took a fistful of cloth in his hand and slashed it until she was free. Snow White looked down at the dress, which now revealed her front and most of her left thigh, cropped so short, she wondered if he saw her undergarments. She glared at him, the heat rising to her face.

The Huntsman narrowed his eyes at her. "Don't flatter yourself, Princess," he grumbled. Then he turned and started running, as if to punish her. She stalled for one second, and he had the lead he needed. She had to sprint to catch up.

As she ran, her entire body was tense, her hands balled

into tight fists. She hated him right then. She hated the smug smile that appeared whenever he was making fun of her, or how he always seemed to know where they were going, even when the entire forest looked the same in every direction. But mostly she hated that she needed him. To lead her, to cut her free from some terrible, man-eating plants. To save her from that bastard Finn.

"Tell me, Huntsman," she gasped once she'd finally caught up. She spit the words at his back. "Do you drink to drown your sorrow or your conscience?"

Eric whipped around, his cheeks flushed from so much grog the night before. "What concern is it of yours why I drink?" He lunged at her, coming just inches from her face.

She didn't flinch. "I believe I have employed you to take me somewhere." She smiled, knowing she had a point.

The Huntsman backed away. He turned and cut at the dense woods with his two axes, swiping at the branches with more force than necessary. A few broken twigs flew at Snow White's face. "And I believe kings and queens and dukes and princesses have no business sticking their noses in common folks' lives."

"But you served the Queen...." She stopped herself, remembering his face in the clearing. He'd grown so quiet when Finn mentioned his wife. "Did she pay you well?" She tried to get back to that conversation. What was the agreement? What had he wanted? The Queen had made a promise even she couldn't keep.

Eric paused, resting his hand on a tree trunk. "Not well

enough," he lied. Then he turned back to his path, bringing his axes down once more. "Royalty does that, you see. They pay others a pittance to fight their battles for them."

Snow White shook her head. She knew he was trying to change the subject, but she no longer cared. Who was he to speak ill of her family? "My father fought his own battles, thank you," she snapped.

The forest opened up before them. The Huntsman lowered his axes. As they started through a dirt clearing, he picked up his pace, trying to lose her. "Your *father*." He let out a smug laugh. "*He's* the one who let the devil in the door. It's *his* fault the kingdom has plunged into darkness."

Snow White jumped over a rotting tree stump. She leveled her gaze at Eric's back, the blood rushing to her face. "Watch your words, Huntsman."

He turned, meeting her glare. "Watch your step." He pointed at her feet. She noticed the dirt was sandier than it was in other places. Her feet were sinking into the ground. First her toes went under, then her ankles, until the sand was nearly up to her shins.

Eric stood there, looking so completely satisfied with himself. "How much does it take for a princess to ask for help?" He laughed. He crossed his arms over his chest, tapping out the seconds with his right foot.

"How much does it take for a brute to offer it?" Snow White snapped back. She tried to free her legs, but it was too late. She'd already sunk down past her knees. The sand felt colder with each inch she went down.

Eric rested one foot on the solid tree stump beside her and offered her his hand. His expression was just a touch softer than before. He lifted her up and out, reaching beneath her arms to get a better grip. When he set her down in the field, she was covered with sand.

She wiped herself off and shook the sand out in the grass. She would have thanked him, but his insults were still fresh in her mind. He hadn't known her father, and he certainly couldn't comprehend what Ravenna was capable of. That woman—that *witch*—had sat beside them at every meal, holding her father's hand. She'd told him about how her mother had grown sick just as Snow White's had. She'd read to Snow White and William when they were bored and thrown parties for the nobility. The king had made a mistake. He'd been fooled. In some ways, they all had.

When she turned back to Eric, he was kneeling in the grass. He handed her some folds of leather. Then he yanked one of the laces from each leather arm brace. He tossed them into her lap.

"You'll freeze to death before we get anywhere. Use these to make some leggings and boots." She held the leather up as a question. "It's the padding from my vest."

Then he picked up a small, dirt-caked nugget from the ground and rolled it between his fingers thoughtfully. "What is that?" she asked, hoping it wasn't what she thought it was.

"A fewmet." He pronounced it *foomay*. "It's from a deer," he replied. He shot her a look, as if to say *please don't make me elaborate*. Snow White watched him knead it

89

between his fingers. Then he brought it to his nose, breathing in its scent. She turned away, disgusted. It must have been droppings.

He stood and pushed past her. He moved quickly, starting toward a patch of trees. The air was different there, the fog so thick she could barely see five feet in front of them.

"Stay here," he said, leaving Snow White behind to fashion some crude clothing for herself.

His stomach had been grumbling all morning. He squeezed the deer dropping between his fingers. Deer didn't usually come inside the Dark Forest, unless they were scared into the trees by another predator. He supposed this morning he'd gotten lucky. Whether the girl was hungry, she hadn't said, but she didn't look as if they had fed her well in the tower.

He kept his eyes on the ground and tracked the animal as he'd done a hundred times before. He moved quickly and quietly, pulling an axe from his waist, ready to throw it should the deer appear. He saw one dropping, then another, as he walked farther into the dense white cloud.

Beyond the fog, the air was clear. There was an outcropping of boulders before him. One opened up to a massive cave. The wind changed, and he heard a familiar voice.

"Eric," she called out from inside the mouth of the cave.

That voice. Hearing it out loud, after so long, raised goose bumps on Eric's skin. He dropped his axe, letting it fall to the earth with a clatter. Sara stepped out of the darkness. She was wearing her favorite dress, the purple fabric more vivid than it ever had been when she was alive. Her dark brown hair framed her face, cascading down her back in thick waves. The full lips he'd kissed a thousand times before were right there in front of him, waiting to be kissed again.

"Are you...?" he asked, glancing down at her body. She was whole again; the wound where she'd been stabbed was gone. There was no gash in her neck.

Eric wiped his eyes. It felt more real than any dream. "Am I...?"

"Touch me and see for yourself," Sara said. She held out her hand, beckoning him toward her.

Eric glanced around, looking beyond the trees. *Don't...* he thought, reminding himself where he was. It was all an illusion now—a picture conjured up by the Dark Forest for some unknown purpose. But as he turned back to Sara, seeing that sweet face again, he couldn't resist. He took a step toward her, closer to the dark cave.

She held out her arms for him. "Where were you, Eric? Come to me now. Protect me now...."

Something inside of him broke. Tears filled his eyes. He remembered the day so clearly, the sight of Sara's body when he finally arrived at the house. Her eyes were open. They were covered with a thin gray film. Her lips were parted. Her hands were cold to the touch. Everything she was—all the joy she'd held inside her—was gone.

"I'm so sorry," Eric whispered. His voice was shaking as he stepped toward her. "Please forgive me. Give me peace...."

She was no more than a few feet away now. He wanted to run his fingertips over her smooth skin. He wanted to hear that sweet, bubbly laugh, to feel her curl up beside him in bed, warming her cold feet against his calves. He wanted to smell the scent of her hair—the lemon juice she put in it during the summer or the rich gardenia oil she dabbed behind her ears.

He reached for her, her fingers nearly touching his, when something struck him in the back of the head. He fell to his knees. He touched the sore spot, wincing from the pain.

"She's not real! *Do you hear me?*" Someone was yelling so loudly, it hurt his ears.

He looked up to see the girl—Snow White—clutching a large stick. She was yelling at him, her face panicked. She pointed at the cave. Eric turned, but the place where Sara had been standing was empty. There, in the darkness, he saw monstrous black wolves huddled together, their long muzzles barely visible in the dim morning light. Their yellow lupine eyes peered out at him. He kicked the ground, shuffling backward, trying to get away.

"She's not real...." Snow White repeated. "She's—"

"I heard you!" Eric yelled. He stared at the place where Sara had stood, just moments before. He'd been so close to touching her. All he wanted was her hand in his, the warmth spreading out between their fingers. He grabbed the bottle by his side and drained it, letting the last of the grog warm his throat. But even that couldn't help him. The tears came fast, and he turned away, making sure the girl didn't see.

They moved quickly through a field of tall, rubbery grass, parting it before them to allow passage. It came up to Snow White's chin. She swatted it away with both hands, but she could only see the back of Eric's head as he reached the other side of the field. He was rubbing the spot where she'd struck him. The blood had dried, clumping in his hair.

She had heard him talking to someone beyond the trees. When she'd found him, his face was tear-streaked and his hands were shaking, one reaching out for something she could not see. "Sara," he'd kept saying as he took another step toward the cave. How had he not seen those monstrous wolves? They were three times the size of normal ones, and their eyes glowed a horrible yellow. How had he not heard their low growling as he'd approached them? They'd been snarling, their upper lips pulled back, exposing their sharp teeth.

Snow White stepped out of the long grass, kicking away the blades that clung to her newly clad legs. She was grateful she had something now to protect them from being sliced into with each slap of the grass.

The Huntsman hadn't turned around since they'd left the cave. He hadn't spoken to her or commented on the apparition he'd seen. He'd just kept moving, cutting at stray branches and bushes with his axe.

"She's the one you bargained for—Sara. The one who spoke to you," Snow White started. She knew he didn't want to talk, but she couldn't pretend it hadn't just happened. Had he seen her there? What kind of illusion had it been? It was clear now his wife wasn't being held captive.... "Is Sara dead?" she asked.

The Huntsman whipped around. He pointed at her with the end of the axe. "You'll not mention her name again," he snapped. Snow White stepped back, her pulse racing. The sharp blade was just two feet away from her neck.

The Huntsman lowered it. "Just don't," he said, his face sad.

He pulled his knife from its sheath and passed it to her, as if to change the subject. She shook her head no, but he pressed it into her hands. "Here—feel its weight. One hand to the other."

She stared at the dagger, noticing that the tip was curved slightly inward. It was heavier than she'd thought it would be. The Huntsman's eyes were fixed on her, watching as she turned it over in her hands, then pointed it toward the ground. "Now hold it—business end pointed toward me."

His face was more serious than before. His straw-colored hair was tucked behind his ears, his beard covered with dirt. She held the knife aloft, the tip of the blade aimed just above his waist. "Why are you—?"

Before she could finish, he lunged at her. She stepped back, raising the blade so it pointed at his throat. He paused just inches away from her. Then he smiled for the first time all day. "Good. Now which is your lead foot?" he asked, circling away. He rested his foot on a nearby tree and studied her.

"What do you mean?" she asked. Behind him, the forest was eerily quiet. Two crows watched them from a low branch. He jumped at her again. Instinctively, she put her right foot forward, not letting him gain any ground this time.

He stalked toward her. She leaned in, the knife in her right hand still pointed at his neck. "Stay back," he said, waving her away, toward the grass field. "You're too small to attack. You have to parry—use your opponent's strength against him. Raise your opposing forearm."

Snow White put her left arm in the air, her wrist parallel to the ground. The Huntsman was still smiling, as if he approved. For the first time since they'd met, she didn't despise him. He seemed kinder now, warm even, as he watched her. He stepped forward again, and this time, Snow White felt the space closing between them. "With it, you'll block and deflect the opposing thrust. You'll lose meat, but you won't die from it," he spoke softly, taking another step. "Wait until I'm close," he urged.

She didn't take her eyes off him. Even though he was moving toward her—the supposed enemy—there was a playfulness in his expression. That dimple appeared again. Her sweaty palm gripped the knife, trying to keep her concentration.

"Not yet," Eric whispered. "Watch my hands, not my eyes."

She lowered her gaze to the axe. His movements were steady as he took another step toward her. She resisted the urge to scare him back with the knife. "Not yet," he repeated. "Not until you can feel my breath."

He took another step, then another, until he was just inches from her. He smiled, his gray eyes daring her to act. She didn't hesitate. She raised the knife, pointing it up, stopping just before it hit his breastbone.

"Yes!" Eric smiled. "That's when you'll drive it through him. To the hilt. Keep your eyes locked on his, and don't pull it out until you see his soul." He wrapped his hand around hers. He held the knife with her, smiling as though she'd done well.

Her breaths were shorter. She pulled her hand away, unsure what it was she felt, with his face so close to hers. "Why are you showing me this?" she asked. "Why now?"

The Huntsman looked over her shoulder. She followed his gaze across the field, to where the caves were. "It's important you know...." He trailed off, not saying what he was suggesting—that he was just as vulnerable to the Dark Forest as she was. "Keep it," he said, nodding to the knife.

Snow White lowered it, sick at the thought of being in the forest alone. As much as she hated to admit it, he was the only thing that comforted her now. He stepped through the trees and started down a narrow path to their left. "Where are you going?" she asked. They were supposed to go north for another mile—he'd said so himself.

He smiled at her, his gray eyes lighting up. He was older than her by five years, maybe more. His hair was knotted, and he stunk of grog. But standing there beside the tree, she saw a flicker of who he might have been before. He seemed calmer—happy, almost.

He pointed to a brown nugget just inches from his feet. "Fewmet." He shrugged.

"Right." Snow White laughed to herself. She hoped he didn't notice the redness in her cheeks. "The fewmet calls."

He started down the short path. Snow White stood there, watching him go, until his back disappeared behind the thick brush.

Ravenna lingered in the cloister garden, rubbing the back of her hand, where the skin looked aged and wrinkled. She closed her eyes for just a moment, and she saw what Finn saw. The visions came in quick flashes—a glimpse of a horse, an open wound in its side. The mercenaries were behind him, slashing through the thick undergrowth with their swords. Somewhere in the Dark Forest, a man screamed, the sound so shrill, it made the hair on her neck stand up.

She had tried to lead Finn over the dangerous terrain despite the limitations of her powers. Now that he was deep in the Dark Forest, she couldn't sense as clearly where he was or whom he was with. The men's faces were featureless. But in the passing hours, she had seen his silhouette cross a bog and move through a dense field of tall, rubbery grass.

He was alive, his shirt covering his mouth and nose as he came out of the stupor caused by the pollen.

The glimpses of the girl were what frightened her. Snow White was with him—that Huntsman—moving toward the forest's edge. She didn't seem hurt or even hindered by the dangerous woods. In only a few hours, they'd emerge from the undergrowth. And what if Finn did not? What if the Dark Forest devoured him as it had done with so many others? Who would retrieve the girl then?

Ravenna started back through the garden, her steps slow and deliberate. The grass was withered and brown. There was only a single blossom on the apple tree, as if the entire castle had been weakened as she had and was now vulnerable to time and death. She stared at the light pink flower, its petals wilting at the edges. It, too, would fall. The bloom would close eventually. The tree would rot from the inside out.

She pressed it between her fingers, twisting the bloom from the dry branch. The thin flower felt so soft and smooth. Then she closed her eyes, trying to harness her powers, leading her brother closer to the girl. "Find her," she whispered as the petals fell apart in her hand.

Eric walked to the edge of the woods, where the thick trees dropped down a steep incline. He signaled for Snow White to follow. Then he shifted both axes to one hip and sat on the other, sliding down the muddy hill. He stumbled to the bottom, the pain shooting through his side. Now that the grog was gone, his wound hurt more than it had before. Every turn and twist felt like another sword ripping through his flesh.

The fog was thinning out. He could barely decipher the structure a hundred feet off, just beyond a pile of large rocks. He moved toward it, climbing onto a boulder to get a better view. A stream snaked its way through the woods. A stone bridge connected both shores. There, beyond it, the Dark Forest finally ended. There were miles of open fields in every direction. "It can't be this easy," he muttered to himself.

He heard Snow White's footsteps approaching behind him. "This is the end of the Dark Forest?" she asked.

Eric turned back to the woods. The massive trees towered above them. "Apparently," he said, glancing at the bridge. This was the right way—he knew it was. He'd tracked the deer to this very spot. But now that they'd arrived, seeing the end of the forest less than a hundred feet away, it was hard to believe they'd made it. It was all over. They'd reached the other side. He looked at Snow White, his face breaking into a grin.

She started past him toward the bridge. She was practically running. "How far to the duke's castle?" she called over her shoulder, her voice light.

Eric ran after her. He combed his hair with his fingers, enjoying the sun on his skin. The Dark Forest was so dense, he hadn't felt it in a while. "Can't be more than five miles straightaway," he said, gesturing to the flock of birds circling on the horizon.

She looked at him and smiled. The late afternoon light streamed through the trees and cast a pink glow on her face. He knew she was beautiful—it was apparent the first time he saw her. But when he looked at her now, he realized she was oblivious to that fact. Though he'd never admit it, in some small way, it made her even more alluring. When she smoothed out the tangles in her hair or narrowed her dark eyes at him, looking as though he were the most dreadful human being alive, there was no playfulness in it. It wasn't some cheap, tavern-girl act.

He rested his hand on his bottom rib, thankful the worst of the journey was over. If he could get her to the village a few miles in, they'd rest there. He'd deliver her to safety—that was enough. He couldn't stick to their agreement. Carmathan was out of the question. In the worst of times, he'd stolen the duke's supplies and traded his men to the Queen's soldiers. It was too shameful to speak of out loud, but it was in the days when a drink mattered more than anything else. As soon as Snow White was safe, he'd disappear into the woods, whether or not she paid him. He'd leave before they faced the duke and his men. He'd be done with all of it—the Queen's nasty business far behind him.

They started over the bridge, their shoulders nearly touching. The field spread out before them. The grass rippled in the wind. Behind him, the bubbling of the creek mixed with a dry, gravelly sound. He glanced back, looking for falling rocks. The bridge appeared to be shifting ever so slightly. The stone crumbled at the sides. Eric rested his hand on Snow White's arm, alerting her. They peered down at the shallow creek. There were hundreds of animal carcasses beneath the surface of the water. He could just make out a bear skull and the freshly chewed rib cage of a giant buck. The bones still glistened with blood.

The bridge started to shake. He knew what it was—the stories of the Dark Forest returned to him all at once. "Troll!" he yelled. The back of the bridge reared up. Eyes opened in the side of the stone. The giant beast had been curled into a ball, just waiting for them to cross. Eric grabbed Snow White's arm and started toward the end of the Dark Forest, but it was still thirty feet away. They'd never make it in time.

The troll stood, sending them flying through the air. Eric slammed down hard in the shallow creek, crushing a broken skeleton under his weight. All the air left his lungs. He lay there, heaving, until he finally caught his breath. His clothes were soaked through, the frigid water sending chills through his entire body. "Are you all right?" he asked, looking for the girl. She'd landed in the muddy bank, her head dangerously close to a sharp rock.

She didn't answer. Instead, she was looking behind him. He turned, following her gaze. The massive creature stood nearly twenty feet tall. Its gray mottled face stared down at them. The top of its head was horned, and its beady eyes were black as coal.

"Run!" Eric yelled, pulling himself onto his feet. Snow White darted out in front of him, and they both took off down the creek bed. The giant followed behind, swinging his fists.

Every time the beast took a step, the earth shook. Eric stumbled to catch his footing, but soon the troll was right behind him.

"Go—get out of here!" he called to the girl. He nodded upstream. If she circled back around, she could be out of the Dark Forest in minutes.

She looked at him, uncertain.

"Just go," he yelled. He pushed her away. Then he spun around, facing the giant monster. The troll stopped, its feet straddling the creek. Eric drew both axes, wielding one in each hand. He didn't have time to think—he just ran at the thing, keeping the axes aimed at its legs.

The troll swung its arm at him. He ducked, and the creature's fist grazed the top of his head. Eric landed both axes in the giant's left leg, but they didn't do any damage. The troll's skin was thick and leathery. The axe blades only nicked it. The monster barely winced.

The giant peered down at him, a low grumbling sound escaping its lips. Then it grabbed Eric by the waist and hurled him down the creek. He slammed into the muddy streambed. He turned onto his side, his head throbbing and his whole body aching from the blow.

The troll started toward him. Eric looked down at his side, which was now covered with blood. The gash below his ribs had reopened. He pressed his hand to it, trying to stop the bleeding.

Within seconds, the troll was hovering over him, its stony face close enough that its hot, rotting breath ruffled his hair. It had yellow teeth that hung over its bottom lip. The giant pulled back its fist. Eric squeezed his eyes shut, waiting for the final blow.

"Get away from him!" the girl screamed. Eric opened his eyes. Snow White was running down the creek, the water splashing up around her ankles. She held out her knife in front of her, just like he'd shown her. It looked so small and pathetic now. It was no bigger than the giant's thumbnail.

"Don't," Eric said under his breath, as if that one word could stop her. His whole body ached. He tried to stand, but the pain shot through his side. The troll stepped away from him, now fixed on Snow White.

The giant started down the creek until it was just a few feet from her. Her eyes were locked on its. She raised her forearm. Even from down the bank, Eric could see she was shaking. He swallowed hard, afraid of what the beast would do. He'd heard how trolls crushed the skulls of their victims before feasting on their innards. He would take his own life before watching the troll take hers.

But the giant just stood there, its eyes narrowing. Each of its breaths was labored, the stench of them making Snow White cringe. The standoff lasted only a few minutes. Then, slowly, it unclenched its fists. The beast leaned forward, its head tilted, taking in the tiny figure before it. Snow White didn't even flinch. She just stared down the huge beast. The troll let out a low snort, then started away from her, back down the creek. It kicked a boulder as it left. Eric watched it all, not sure if it had really happened.

When the troll was out of sight, Snow White finally lowered her knife. She ran to Eric and threw her arms around his sides. Slowly, she helped him to his feet.

Eric shook his head. He couldn't believe she'd been so reckless. The troll could have snapped her neck with a flick of its finger. "I told you to run," he said, searching her brown eyes.

Her face hardened. "If I had, you'd be dead. A 'thank you' would suffice." She let him go, and he stumbled back, trying to catch his balance. Then she turned, starting up the rocky shore alone.

"Wait," he said softly. He stared at the girl. A lock of black hair fell in her eyes. She had a scrape across her forehead, but otherwise she was unharmed. He kept watching her, this hundred-and-ten-pound nothing, wondering what had made her so strong. Why had she risked it? What had made her turn back, with only a five-inch blade to defend her? He'd met grown men with less fight in them.

Snow White crossed her arms over her chest. "What?" she said, an edge in her voice.

He smiled, slowly walking up to her. He rested his hand on her shoulder, not taking his eyes off her. "Thank you."

Part Two

And only by fairest blood

can it be
undone...

They trekked three miles across the field, through another copse of trees, to where the land opened up to a marsh. Snow White removed her make-shift leather shoes and let her bare feet sink into the mud. She trudged forward, one step at a time, Eric following behind her.

He'd said this was the way to Carmathan. He'd told her to keep going, through the marsh. But with every mile marked, she grew more suspicious. The duke's stronghold wasn't visible in the distance. She saw no signs of his men. She thought only of that map in the dirt, and that village Eric had pointed to—the place he'd initially wanted to take her.

The water rose. Snow White held up the hem of her dress—what was left of it, anyway—trying to stay dry. Her feet squished through the wet earth, the cold mud between her toes. She watched the tiny fish swim around her ankles.

Whole schools of them came toward her, then darted away, moving as she moved. When she finally looked up, she noticed the dark figures up ahead. They stood on the bank of the marsh, nearly thirty feet away. They were silhouetted against the setting sun, but she could just make out the bows and arrows slung over their backs.

It was too late to turn around. Snow White kept her head down, hoping they wouldn't recognize her. As they approached, one of the figures stepped forward, face hidden by a black hood. The person aimed an arrow at Snow White's chest. "They say only demons or spirits can survive the Dark Forest. Which are you?"

Eric pulled his hatchets from his waist and stepped in front of Snow White, putting himself between her and the cloaked figure.

"Perhaps you are the Queen's spies?" the person went on.

"We're fugitives from the Queen," Eric offered.

Snow White looked up, letting the cloaked figure see her face. "We mean you no harm," she tried. She rested her hand on Eric's arm, signaling for him to lower the hatchets. He obliged.

Then the figure leaned back, letting the hood fall away. For the first time, Snow White could see the person was a woman. Her red hair was twisted back in braids. She had small, delicate features—a narrow nose and high cheek-bones. But her most distinguishing feature was her scar. The thick, pink line ran from the top of her forehead over her eye, then down her right cheek, stopping just above her chin.

The others lowered their weapons. They took off their hoods, too. They were all women, and they were all beautiful. But they all had identical scars, in the exact same spot, cutting down the right sides of their faces. "Where are the men?" Eric asked.

"Gone," the woman with the red hair replied. Then she smiled, reaching out her hand for Snow White to take. "I'm Anna," she said. "Welcome."

A few hours later, Snow White sat by a fire, a wool blanket draped over her shoulders. She was wearing dry, clean clothes for the first time in years. The pants were a little too big, and the shirt was rough against her skin, but she'd never felt so luxurious.

She watched as one of the older women from the village stitched up Eric's wound. The woman bandaged it with clean linen, tying the gauze in place before leaving. Eric looked calmer than she'd ever seen him before. His face was soft in the firelight.

The village was a series of thatch huts on stilts, the shallow water passing underneath. Anna had taken them by boat to her home, which was twenty feet above the marshland and surrounded by a wooden platform. Now she sat on the corner of the deck with her daughter. The little girl was no more than seven years old. The two worked slowly, gutting fish, then hanging them on a piece of twine to dry.

"This is the village, isn't it?" Snow White said, turning to Eric. She already knew the answer. "The one you aimed to bring me to before you *swore* to take me to the duke's castle?"

Eric lowered his eyes. "I'm not sure how warm a welcome I'd get at Hammond's." He pulled his shirt back on, wincing as it slid over his sides.

"Why?" Snow White asked. She crossed her arms over her chest, waiting for the excuse. He had lied to her. He'd said he'd take her to the duke's castle and he hadn't—it was as simple as that.

Eric sighed. He leaned forward, holding his scraped hands up to the fire. "I may have bountied a few of the duke's rebels along the way. I steal from the duke, he steals from the Queen—cycle of life kind of thing."

Snow White nearly laughed. He'd said it so casually, with no remorse. She'd never met someone so devoid of feeling. "I'll go to the duke's with or without you."

Eric met her gaze. "I kept my word. I promised I'd deliver you to safety. This is safe, right?" He glanced at the huts across from them. Each one had a small fire burning on the wooden porch. Women sat with one another, some eating, others talking about Snow White's arrival.

Snow White looked down at her hands. They were still filthy from the Dark Forest. Dirt was encrusted beneath each nail, even though she had washed them in Anna's basin. When she glanced up, Eric was staring at her. He held something in his palm. "What is that?" she asked.

"It's made of gristle from a stag's heart." She shrugged, not sure what the significance was. He continued. "The stag is the most timid animal in the forest. But there's a bone in its heart. Some say it gives it courage in its hour of need. It's a protection charm." As Eric said it, his eyes misted over. He spoke so slowly and deliberately, as if trying to maintain control over his emotions. Snow White instinctively knew it had been a gift from Sara.

He shook his head and laughed. "Doesn't work, though." He smirked, tucking the object back in his pocket.

As he did, Anna strode over, a plate of fish in her hands. She set the metal down on the fire and let it simmer. The smell of trout filled the air. Snow White glanced back at her daughter, Lily, who continued cutting the remaining fish. She had huge blue eyes and full cheeks. Even though she was scarred like the others, Snow White couldn't look away.

"She's beautiful," she finally said.

Anna's long red hair had come loose and fell around her face in tight waves. She rubbed at her forehead. "That is not a kind thing to say in these times. The compliment becomes a curse. Youth, one cannot alter, beauty however..."

Snow White's eyes welled up at the thought of mothers scarring their children so they wouldn't become victims of the Queen. All this so Ravenna wouldn't do to them what she'd done to Rose. "It makes me very sad," she said.

Anna looked from Eric back to Snow White. "We have sacrificed beauty to raise our children in peace. And you, your sacrifice will come, Princess."

Snow White looked at Eric accusingly. He shook his

head. "Don't look at me," he said, throwing up his hands. "I didn't say anything."

Anna tilted her head. "I know who you are. There was news of your escape. Two rebel leaders from Carmathan were caught by the Queen the same day you left the castle. One survived and returned to the duke." She reached out and took Snow White's hand in hers. "Prepare yourself, my dear. For a time soon comes when you must deliver that sacrifice and rule this kingdom."

"How do you know that?" Snow White said. She pulled her hand away from Anna's, uncertain of this woman. They'd known each other for only a few hours. No matter how much the woman had helped them, she was still a stranger. How could she speak to Snow White this way?

Anna looked at Snow White. "I can feel it." She stood and returned to Lily, helping her finish the rest of the fish.

Snow White felt her cheeks burning. Anna didn't know what she was saying. Why did it matter what she felt? Snow White wasn't a warrior. She would go to Duke Hammond's and stay there until the war ended. Women had never fought in the army before. It wasn't allowed.

Snow White lay down on the deck, wrapping the wool blanket around her. She tried to sleep, but she could feel Eric watching her. "What?" she finally asked when she couldn't stand it any longer.

Eric smiled at her. "Nothing, Princess," he said softly. Then he pulled the fish from the fire, picking the flesh off its bones.

He thought about what Anna had said. Somehow, it didn't surprise him. The way Snow White had saved him in the Dark Forest meant something. She had a will inside her that others didn't. Whether Anna could *feel* it, as she had said, was a whole different story.

He watched as the girl finally gave in to sleep. Anna and her daughter retired in the thatch hut, offering a quiet good-night. He stayed there for a long while, all the fires dying down around him. Soon he was alone in the dark.

The Queen would be coming for him soon. He had escaped with her prisoner, betrayed her men, and wounded her brother. It wouldn't be long before she tracked him to the woods beyond the Dark Forest. Now that death was coming, he resisted it, not wanting it to happen this way— on *her* terms. Not after she had lied.

Although it was possible that Anna had imagined the whole "your sacrifice will come" scenario, it was just the excuse he needed. Snow White would be fine on her own. She had saved him twice in the Dark Forest. She had the knife and was smart enough to get to the duke's stronghold on her own. It would take the Queen's men another day to get around the Dark Forest—at least.

He gathered his things in the dark, tucking the hatchets back into his belt. He grabbed extra linen for his wound and another trout for the day ahead. Then he looked down at Snow White's face one last time. Her lips were moving in sleep.

"Dammit," he muttered, hating that it wasn't as easy as

he'd hoped. He wasn't one for connections or relationships, all the complications that came when you got used to having someone in your life. It was always easier on his own.

He started toward the ladder on the other side of the hut. Then he stopped, feeling the weight of the locket charm in his trousers pocket. He turned it over in his hand, remembering the day Sara had given it to him. It was after the battles had started. There was news of men getting killed in the forest. Robbers looted supply wagons and torched the roads. "Just in case," she'd said, pressing it into his palm. She'd always been superstitious that way.

He looked at it one last time, knowing that Sara would've wanted the girl to have it. She would've liked her spirit, the way she always seemed to be thinking something she wouldn't share. And Sara would have been thankful for what the girl had done that day, the courage she'd shown at the edge of the Dark Forest. Although he hated to admit it, he was, too.

He rested the locket in the girl's open palm, hoping that what Sara had said was right. Maybe it *did* work. Maybe it *wasn't* a complete joke. He was alive, wasn't he? He had survived losing her, despite his careless regard for his own life. He'd made it through the Dark Forest. Something had been protecting him all these years.

"Just in case," he said quietly. Then he started down the ladder, not daring to look back.

There was a scream. Snow White awoke, her eyes
slowly adjusting to the dark. It took her a moment
to realize where she was. The fire had gone out.
Pressed inside her palm was a bone locket—the
same one Eric had held hours before. She looked around the
wooden deck, searching the inside of the thatch hut, where
Anna and Lily slept. The Huntsman was gone.

She looked out and scanned the village. The air was
filled with smoke. The raised house across the way glowed
with an eerie light. Two of the women peered out from the
small window in its side, one covering her mouth in horror.
Snow White circled the deck, finally seeing what they saw.
The sky was filled with flaming arrows. Archers stood on
the hillside above the village, silhouetted by the gray star-
lit sky.

Within seconds, the first arrow struck. The fiery missile
buried itself in the thatch house just two away from Anna's.

The roof caught fire, the flames spreading out from where it hit, consuming the tiny structure in minutes. The older woman who'd bandaged Eric's wound ran out of the hut. Her thin linen dress had caught fire in the back. She reached over her shoulder, trying to smack it out, but it was no use. As she ran, the flames grew, her hair catching fire. She screamed as she jumped off the wooden deck, extinguishing herself in the marsh below.

Finn's army was coming closer. Snow White could see their faces now, glowing in the firelight as they approached the banks of the marsh. Some led their horses through the shallow waters. They kept shooting up into the houses. Others climbed into the boats on shore, pushing off into the still water. Far below, a man with a knife jumped onto the wooden ladder and began climbing up to the thatch hut. A woman with a long black braid threw firewood on him from the deck above, trying to slow his progress.

Then Snow White spotted him. Finn led his horse out from behind the trees. He raised his bow, launching an arrow into a nearby hut. "Find her!" he yelled.

Snow White slipped behind the hut, careful not to be seen. She moved quickly. "They're here!" she yelled, darting into the thatch room. She raced toward Anna, shaking her awake. "The Queen's men are here."

Anna rubbed her eyes. She looked at Snow White in disbelief. As she sat up, an arrow came through the roof, lodging in the thin mattress beside Lily's head. The wool blanket caught on fire. Snow White raced toward the sleeping girl, pulling her from the bed and heaving her over her shoulder. She was about to run when Anna screamed.

Snow White spun around. Behind her, standing right on the deck, was one of Finn's men. He smiled when their eyes met, revealing a missing front tooth. He was so tall and broad that he filled the entire doorway, making it impossible to pass through. Then, without any warning, he charged.

Before she could think, she yanked the arrow out of the mattress and jammed the flaming tip into his thigh, not stopping until it met bone. He let out an excruciating cry. Then he toppled over, the flames spreading to his calves and waist until the whole lower half of his body was burning. He twisted in pain.

Snow White watched him, horrified. She couldn't stop staring at his scrunched-up face. Water squeezed out of the corners of his eyes. The hut filled with the putrid stink of burning flesh. She doubled over, the smoke caught in her lungs. For a moment, she was afraid she'd be sick.

Anna grabbed her arm. "Come on," she yelled, nodding to the door. Snow White started out, turning back one last time to see the soldier. He'd curled onto his side. He was heaving, his hands trying to subdue the growing flames.

They took the ladder down, nearly two rungs at a time. Snow White splashed into the marsh, Lily over her shoulder. The little girl started crying as they started through the muddy water, which came up to Snow White's chest. There was chaos all around them. Many of the stilted houses were on fire. Smoke and ash filled the air. Pieces of burning debris fell from above, plunging into the shallow marsh water, extinguished with a hiss.

Anna pointed to the shore fifty feet off. A few of the women had already reached it and now sprinted into the trees. Snow White followed her through the mud, moving as fast as she could. Behind them, they heard the shouts and cries of the other women. A girl who was younger than Lily held her mother's hand as they jumped from the wooden deck. Snow White kept her eyes on the bank ahead, not wanting to look back. "Where is she?" one of the men called out.

When they finally reached the shore, their clothes were soaked through. Snow White started ahead, following the rest of the women, when a horse cut across her path. One of the mercenaries jumped down from it. The man was heavier than the others, with a chin that spilled over the top of his shirt. He unsheathed his sword and stalked toward her.

"Run!" Snow White cried, passing Lily into Anna's arms. Snow White pointed to the thick woods. If she distracted him, they'd have enough time to get away. She stepped out front to where the man could see her clearly. She held the knife in her right hand, taking the stance the Huntsman had shown her, one arm up and the other still, just waiting for the enemy to come close.

The mercenary came at her. She held the knife aloft, looking into his black eyes. *One* ... she thought, watching him near, *two* ... *three*. When he was just inches away, she slashed at him with the knife. He stumbled back, a small wound opening in his chest. He threw his head back and laughed. Then he punched her hard in the stomach. She fell to the ground. She opened her mouth, but she couldn't take in air.

He raised his sword. She stared up at him, gasping for breath, waiting for the blade to come down on her neck. Then an arrow whizzed past, hitting him just above his heart. He let out a horrible scream as he stumbled backward. He dropped his sword, instead pulling at the feathered end of the arrow, trying to get it out.

Snow White sat up. Standing just ten feet away was a young soldier, the bow still in his hands. He was tall and thin, with a square jaw and high cheekbones. He had thick, wavy brown hair that fell into his eyes and a subtle cleft in his chin. He stood there, watching her, a slight smile on his lips. She noticed the way he pushed the bow over his shoulder so it was slung across his back. There was something so familiar about that gesture. She recognized him—but from where?

The smoke rose up around them. The fire had spread to some of the trees. The women screamed as they took off toward the hills. The young man opened his mouth to speak, but Anna ran forward, grabbing Snow White by the arm.

"Come on!" she hissed. "There's not much time." She pointed to the muddy banks, where Finn's men were starting up the hill, following them.

They turned and ran. A flaming arrow landed in the

ground beside them. Somewhere in the distance, a child was crying, the sobs sending chills through Snow White's body. She followed Anna through the woods, running as fast as her legs could carry her. She glanced over her shoulder one last time, into the burning trees, but the boy was gone.

Snow White ran so fast she could barely breathe. She recognized that boy in the woods. She knew him from somewhere. And from the way he'd looked at her, she was certain he'd recognized her, too. But how?

She moved through the trees, her hand clutching the knife. Anna was right behind her. Snow White could hear her feet pounding the earth. She thought again of that memory from so long ago. The little boy who'd climbed the apple tree with her, how his toy bow hung from his back. William. She'd seen traces of him in the young man's face. They shared the same hazel eyes, the same smile. It finally hit her and she knew it was him. He was alive after all these years. But what was he doing in the village? How had he found her?

Snow White paused, glancing over her shoulder to look frantically for him once more. Anna and Lily had fallen back. Anna was hunched over a tree trunk, pulling a thorn from Lily's bare foot. The little girl was crying. Behind them, Snow White could see the destruction. The fire had spread. Most of the stilted houses were up in flames. Women darted through the trees. Melva, a young girl with freckles, flew past, clutching what was left of her belongings.

Then Snow White spotted Finn stalking up the bank, looking directly at her. "There!" he yelled to another soldier. He gestured for the mercenary to circle around.

Snow White turned to run, but someone grabbed her from behind. She slashed the air with a knife until she heard a familiar voice. "This way," the Huntsman said. He pointed to a narrow path between trees. It snaked over the hill, to the east of the Dark Forest. "Come on!" Eric hissed.

"We have to help them!" She struggled against his grasp, trying to get to Anna and Lily. Maybe the Huntsman had abandoned them, but she couldn't. She broke free and ran back, helping Anna up from the dirt.

Anna pushed her away. "You will," she said. She pointed down the bank, to where Finn was less than fifty feet away. "Now go."

Snow White looked into her face, realizing that Anna was serious. A mercenary was sprinting through the trees to their left. Finn was closing in. Snow White grabbed the Huntsman's hand, and he pulled her through the woods, maneuvering down the dark path until the scene disappeared behind the thick undergrowth.

They darted through the trees. They covered mile upon mile, circling the shore of a giant lake, then moving east, to where the forest thinned out. As the sun came up, the sounds of the battle were far behind them. Snow White finally stopped, her legs too tired to go any farther. She knelt down on the bank of a shallow stream.

Her hands were still trembling. She plunged them into the cold water, working the dried blood from her fingernails. The smell of smoke clung to her. She heard the women screaming even though the forest was calm, and the birds were silent above. She turned to the Huntsman, hating him right then. He'd *left* them. He'd slunk away in the black of night and left them. The women were defenseless against Finn's men.

"Why did you come back?" she asked, standing to look him in the eye. "Why?"

Eric covered his face with his hands. "I led them there," he said quietly. He was the one who'd brought Snow White to their village. He'd misjudged. He'd thought Finn's men were farther off. Then, as he'd climbed the hill to leave, he'd seen the first arrow fly. He could smell the smoke, even a mile off.

"*I* am the one to blame." His throat was tight, each word hard to get out. He should never have left her. It was just as it had been with Sara. He'd made a choice, and when he'd returned, it was already too late.

He covered Snow White's hands with his. They were shaking. Her face was streaked with ash, and there was dry blood spatter on her arm—from what, he didn't know. "I'll take you to Duke Hammond's," he said. Whatever he faced at the duke's castle couldn't be worse than what he felt now, seeing her like this.

She nodded, but said no more. He lay down on the bank, listening for the sound of hoofbeats in the forest. They could rest here for a few minutes—but not much more. The men would find their trail eventually. He closed his eyes, the exhaustion setting in. His body ached from the past few days. The wound in his side throbbed, the stitches pinching the skin. He felt more now without the grog. That hollow, numb feeling was gone. Was that a blessing or a curse? He couldn't decide.

He looked up, watching the sunlight flicker through the trees. A shadow passed over him. He tried to stand when someone kicked him hard in the side. Another person nailed him in the face. He caught glimpses of small figures coming at him, some punching him, others rapping him with tree branches. They all wore carved wooden battle masks.

"Dwarves," he muttered, knowing at once who they were. He tried to get to Snow White, but one of the nasty little things tied a rope around his ankles. Within seconds, he was being dragged across the bank. They strung him up by the legs. The world spun around him as he hung there, all the blood rushing to his face.

When he finally stopped spinning, he noticed Snow White on the ground beside him. Her arms were tied behind her back. The dwarves were lined up in front of him. They pushed their grotesque battle masks up onto their foreheads.

"Well, well, well…the miscreant Huntsman," Beith said. He was the leader of them all and the nastiest, to boot. His thick black hair came down in front, forming a giant V on his head.

"Come on, Beith." Eric tried to laugh, narrowing his eyes at the little runt. "Is this how you treat a friend?" Anyone who'd traveled through the kingdom knew the dwarves. They hid in the woods, often getting drunk, ready to pick a fight with anyone who was willing. Eric was *always* willing.

Beith lunged at him, so close Eric could smell the toad guts on his breath. "No, you horn beast." He grabbed a thick branch from off the ground. "*This* is how I treat a friend!" He struck him hard in the head.

"Stop it!" Snow White screamed. But the dwarves just chuckled.

Eric held his head in his hands, rubbing the tender spot where Beith had hit him. The little rodents were no more than three feet tall—stocky, stinky men with tangled hair and rotting teeth. Beith had a knotted black beard and clothes that were too big. His pants were held up with an old piece of rope. Eric spotted Muir, the blind dwarf, in the back. Nion was right beside him. He was the most spiteful of all. If it were up to him, the whole world would've been run by dwarves, with the tallsters there only to serve.

Snow White worked at the rope around her wrists. "What did you do to them?" she whispered as the men consulted one another about Eric.

Eric rubbed his face. He was getting dizzy. Everything looked strange upside down. "I tried to collect a bounty on their heads...a few times."

The girl rolled her eyes at him. "Is there no one you haven't wronged?"

He glanced at her, loving the way her nose scrunched up when she was angry. Technically there *was* one person—her. He would've said as much had Beith not turned and started after him, punching him hard in the stomach.

"This is my lucky day!" Beith yelled. "The puttock I loathe most in the world lands in my lap."

"It is your lucky day, Beith," Eric said, trying to sound light. Finn's men would be here soon. He didn't have time to argue about who had tried to sell whom to the Queen. Those were *minor* details. "I've got enough gold to keep you in ale for a year. Cut me down, and I'll—"

Nion clapped him on the ear. "Shut your ugly mug, Huntsman. You had any pennies, they would've fallen out of your pockets by now." Eric clutched his head, which was throbbing now. The ringing hurt too much.

Eric let out a loud grunt. "Just tell me what I've done wrong."

"Tell me what you've done *right* first," Beith replied. Spit flew from his mouth as he spoke. Behind him, the youngest dwarf, Gus, was staring at Snow White as if she was the most beautiful woman he'd ever seen. He smiled, revealing his crusty yellow teeth.

Eric pointed to the girl. "I saved her from the Queen."

Beith shook his head. "Doesn't sound like you, Huntsman."

"People change," Eric tried.

Nion smacked him on the ear again. "*People*—not rut-tish swine."

A few of the other dwarves broke out into an argument. Coll and Duir, who were always fighting with each other, went back and forth, trying to decide if they should kill Eric or leave him tied up, waiting to die.

"Let's skewer him and leave her to rot!" Duir suggested. Eric hated the gleeful tone in his voice.

"No!" a voice called out from behind them. Muir, the elderly dwarf, came forward. His eyes were covered in a thin white film. "She is destined," he continued. He held up one finger to silence them.

Eric remembered the blind man from another visit in the woods. The others listened when he spoke.

Beith turned back to the girl, studying her with a new curiosity.

"Do you hate the Queen?" Snow White asked, seizing the opportunity. "My father was King Magnus."

The group settled down. Eric watched the girl, amused. It was the same boldness she'd shown in the Dark Forest. He was beginning to wonder if there was anyone she *wouldn't* challenge.

Beith tilted his head to one side.

"If you accompany us to the duke's castle, you will be paid handsomely," Snow White went on. "Your weight in gold. Each of you."

Duir looked Coll up and down, taking in his spindly arms and legs. "I get more than you," he whispered, smacking his fat belly.

"True," Coll replied. He stifled a heavy cough. "But

because of your size, you eat more and drink more, which costs more, so—"

"All right," Beith interrupted. "We'll take you, but the Huntsman can hang." He cleared his throat, then hocked a giant glob of phlegm in the dirt beside Eric's head.

"Both of us," the girl said. She glanced sideways at Eric and nodded, as if to reassure him.

Beith stroked his black beard as if he was considering it. As they waited, Duir, one of the dwarves Eric had tried to sell, pointed to a spot on the horizon. Eric followed his gaze, noticing the silhouettes coming over the hill. It was Finn and the mercenaries. They were coming for them. "Those are the Queen's men, Beith," Eric said. He twisted and kicked, trying to free his feet. "Better decide quickly."

"One dwarf's worth a dozen tallsters," Beith snapped. "I'll take my time, thank you." But then Beith glanced up at the hill. Ten more men appeared on horseback, their swords drawn. A few of the dwarves shrank away, already running from the sight.

"You were saying?" Eric asked, narrowing his eyes at the little man. He could barely see anymore. All the blood had rushed to his head, making his temples throb.

"Cut him down," Beith said, signaling to Nion. "Move out!"

Gus helped Snow White out of her restraints. Nion freed Eric with one slash of his knife. Then they started down the hill, Eric and Snow White following behind the dwarves, crouching low to avoid being seen.

Snow White glanced up at the cave's giant dome. Mineral water dripped down the rock walls. A thin stream of light came in from a hole in the ceiling, highlighting the clusters of bats hanging side by side, their wings folded around them. The thuds of hoofbeats sounded above. Finn's army shouted across the forest. "I found a rope!" one man yelled. Then the horses changed direction, galloping off until the woods were silent again.

Duir and Coll pointed to a long tunnel in the side of the cave, signaling for the rest of them to follow. The dwarves filed in. They fit easily into the narrow passageway. Snow White hunched over, trying to make herself as small as possible, but her elbows still grazed the walls. She glanced over her shoulder, watching as the Huntsman shuffled in sideways.

The dwarves had led them under a giant tree root and into the cave, helping them escape Finn's men. They knew the underground labyrinth well. They weaved through the crisscrossing maze of tunnels, taking turn after turn, until they were deep in the earth. Snow White looked down at the wooden rail tracks beneath her feet, realizing it was a mine. She tried to think about just putting one foot in front of another, and not... *William. Where is he?* She kept trudging along after the dwarves until, suddenly, the tunnel opened up to a green pasture.

Outside, the light was so intense, she shielded her eyes. A shimmering landscape spread out before her. Every color of flower sprouted up from the earth—lush yellow daisies, blooming hydrangeas, and exotic pink rosebuds—filling the air with the most intoxicating fragrance. And then there was the sound, an enchanting humming noise that swelled in her ears, making her want to dance.

"Blasted fairy music," Nion grumbled. He plunged his fingers into the thick moss that coated the rocks, grabbing a whole fistful. He shaped some plugs and stuffed them into his ears.

Snow White looked around, taking in the dazzling scenery. Flowering vines wrapped around the massive trees, covering them in lush purple blooms. Red and gold butterflies settled on their limbs. Rabbits bounded through the tall grass, darting this way and that. All in front of her, tiny bulbs of pollen hung in the air. The glittering particles caught the light, making it look like even the air sparkled.

"What is this place?" she asked, trying to catch the tiny specks in her hands.

Gus ran to her side. "They call it Sanctuary, my lady," he said, looking up at her with his big, watery gray eyes. He smiled, revealing his crooked yellow teeth. She hated to admit it, but the little guy was growing on her. "The Enchanted Forest. It's the home of the fairies."

Snow White turned to the Huntsman, who was just as stunned as she was. He opened his mouth to speak, but something whizzed past his head, startling them both. Snow White studied the tiny fairy hovering just two feet away. It had translucent white skin and ears that were pointed at the top, and its iridescent blue wings shimmered in the sunlight. It looked at her and smiled before zipping away, leaving a dense trail of pollen in its wake.

"Fairies," Gus said sweetly. He reached out to hold Snow White's hand.

Gort kicked through the tall grass. He was the heaviest of all the men, with a full belly that hung over his belt. "Pests!" he snorted. Then the dwarves dispersed into the forest to set up camp for the night.

Snow White and the Huntsman helped cut down fire-wood, while Coll and Duir cleared away the tall grass and broken branches, leaving a patch of dirt for them to lie down on. Beith retrieved some supplies they kept hidden in tangled tree roots, creating a heaping pile of flagons, dented pots, and dried fox meat. There was even a weathered fiddle. When the dwarves finally settled down around the fire, Gus tucked the fiddle under his chin and began to play.

"Play louder, you whey-face!" Gort yelled. "I can still

hear those harpy fairies." He covered his ears with both hands. Across the way, Muir sat with his son Quert, resting his hand on the young dwarf's shoulder. Duir and Coll were swigging ale, their movements loose as they gestured wildly, absorbed in another one of their arguments. Snow White sat beside Eric, watching the dwarves tumble around, pushing one another as they danced a wild dance.

Eric chuckled to himself. "Legend has it, dwarves were created to uncover all the riches hidden on earth. Not just gold or precious stones, but the beauty in people's hearts."

Snow White stared at him, wondering if the phrase *the beauty in people's hearts* had really just come out of his mouth. She looked down at Eric's side. There were a few fox bones, but no bottle of rum or grog. She stared into his face, noticing for the first time that his eyes were clear. He spoke slowly and carefully, choosing his words. It had been two days, at least, and he hadn't drunk a thing.

Eric pointed at Nion. The dwarf was stumbling around, belting a tune in Gort's ears so loudly the dwarf cringed. "Ask me, they've lost the art if they ever had it. When the Queen seized their mines, she didn't just take their treasure— she stole their pride."

Snow White surveyed the men. Most were drunk. Coll and Duir wrestled on the ground, pressing each other's faces into the dirt. Gus danced as he played the fiddle, sweat pouring down the sides of his face. It was hard to imagine any magic within them. How could they bring out the best in people when they seemed so unhappy themselves?

As Quert stepped up to sing a more cheerful song, Muir started over to them. Gort held the blind dwarf's hand, helping him to an old tree stump, where he sat down to rest. The dwarf had long gray hair and a wrinkled face. He had to be at least twenty years older than the others. Snow White rested her hand on his knee so he'd know she was there. "Thank you for before," she said softly. "For defending me."

Muir nodded. "Your father was a good man. The kingdom prospered then. Our people prospered."

"There were more of you?" Snow White asked. Muir nodded.

Gort leaned back onto the tree stump and took another swig of his drink. "One day, the group you see before you went down into the mine for a monthlong shift. Gus was only a boy. When we came back to the surface...nothing. The land was black. Everything and everyone was dead. Gone." He snapped his fingers to show how quickly it had happened.

"That was a month after your father died," Muir added. Snow White nodded. She remembered that first month, too. She'd heard the explosions out beyond the castle walls. Fires burned the countryside. Ravenna's soldiers hooted in the courtyard, bragging about the villages they'd torched and the deaths they'd avenged. She was only seven years old then, but she knew that the kingdom would never be the same. She had felt it in the pit of her stomach. *She* would never be the same.

They sat there, Muir by her side, until the sun set in the west. Snow White danced to a happier tune with Gus, letting the young dwarf step on her toes. She sang with Nion and ate the remnants of the fox meat, enjoying her first real meal in some days. But at the end of the night, as the dwarves drifted off to sleep, she couldn't stop thinking of what Muir had said back in the woods. *She is destined.* It was the future that Anna had foretold, how she would sacrifice herself and lead the kingdom. When the words had come out of Anna's mouth they'd seemed so strange. She'd spent her life as a prisoner of the Queen, locked inside the castle tower. How could she lead anyone? And even if she tried, why would anyone listen?

She thought of Anna's village, how the women had all fled into the woods, their homes engulfed in flames. Lily couldn't stop crying. Now, after all that Snow White had seen, Anna's prophecy was easier to believe. She couldn't watch Ravenna's men take another life. She didn't want to hear the cries of women who'd lost their homes, or see the scarred faces of children who were slashed just so the Queen wouldn't take them from their mothers.

She glanced around the dense forest. Flowers grew around the Huntsman, whose face looked calmer—handsome even—when he slept. Coll and Duir dozed back to back, as if they were forever joined. As the night took hold, more creatures emerged from the dense forest—squirrels, beavers, and colorful birds that swooped down out of the trees.

Two magpies fluttered in front of her face, their iridescent wings shimmering in the moonlight. They transformed in a split second, turning into fairies. She stared at them, realizing that they had been the two who'd helped her when she was locked in the castle. They were the ones who'd saved her.

They darted away, waving for her to follow. Their sweet humming filled the air. She started through the woods to where a bright white light shone in the darkness, just beyond a pile of stone ruins. As she approached, the magic of the forest showed itself. The animals surrounded her, moving as she did through the towering trees. Birds flew in formations above. Rabbits and deer came out from the woods, following in a massive group behind her.

It wasn't until she was just ten feet away that she could see where the light was coming from. A majestic white stallion stood beneath a giant tree. The air around the creature glowed with a magical gold light.

Snow White approached the giant horse. It leaned down, letting her stroke its cheek. Its dark brown eyes stared back at her, as if it understood everything she was thinking and feeling. He pressed his head against hers. She could feel the animal's warm breath on her neck. She turned back to the forest, noticing for the first time that the dwarves and the Huntsman had awoken and followed her. They all fanned out behind her, watching the scene through the trees.

Beith shook his head in disbelief. "No one's ever seen it before," he said.

"It is blessing her," Muir offered from beyond the

glowing woods. "She is life itself. She will heal the land. She is the one."

Snow White wrapped her hands around the animal's neck and felt the deepest peace. Listening to the prophecy now, here, she was filled with the desire to act. She would do whatever the kingdom asked of her. She would restore dignity to the throne.

As she pet the horse, the light glowed brighter. Shimmering gold particles floated around them, engulfing her. "Gold or no gold," Muir said to the other men. "Where she leads, I follow."

Snow White smiled and rested her head against the stallion's neck. As she went to pet its beautiful white coat, she saw it out of the corner of her eye. An arrow whizzed through the air. It came from up above, piercing the creature's tender flank. The gentle animal reared in pain, then bolted off through the forest, nearly toppling her. All the other animals scattered. The dwarves turned, their weapons drawn. On the hill above them were Finn's men, their swords drawn.

A fierce wind whipped through the trees, dispersing dark shadows where there once was light. The dwarves pulled on their battle masks and grabbed their weapons. Eric drew his hatchets from his belt, wielding one in each hand. Snow White sized up Finn's men, scanning the face of each one. Then she froze, staring into the hazel eyes she'd known as a child. William was beside them. He was on his horse, his sword drawn. Why was he here now? Why was he fighting *with* them?

There wasn't any time to process it. The brute who'd shot the white horse raised his bow, notching another arrow. He aimed it at her and smiled. Before she could move, William knocked the man from his horse, sending the arrow flying into the treetops. Gus grabbed her hand and pulled her into the forest, away from the men. "Come on!" he yelled as Finn's army descended on them.

The humming of the enchanted forest was replaced with battle cries. Swords clanked together. The horses whinnied behind them. Snow White kept running, Gus by her side. She glanced back over her shoulder. William maneuvered his horse through the trees. He followed close behind, his armor glinting in the moonlight.

Gus pulled ahead of her, his hand squeezing her fingers so hard they hurt. "Faster!" he yelled, jumping over fallen branches and rocks. But Snow White kept her eyes on William. He was twenty feet behind them, maybe more. She broke free of Gus's grip and darted into the bushes, waiting there until William was within reach. As soon as he rode past, she jumped up and grabbed his arm with both hands. Then she yanked him back, sending him tumbling off the horse.

Gus ran to her. He drew his axe, ready to bring it down on William's neck. "Gus, don't!" Snow White yelled. Gus slowed his axe just in time. It stopped mere inches from William's skin.

She hovered over him, staring into the face she remembered from a decade before. His wavy brown hair stuck up in a hundred directions, just as it had when he was a kid. "What are you doing?" she asked. "I saw you in the village."

"It's me," he said. "William." He sat up, his chest heaving. He picked his bow off the ground and gathered the arrows in one hand.

"I know," Snow White said, her voice tight. She could barely believe it. The boy she'd imagined all those years had returned. He had cried for her that night, the night they'd ridden away. But was he here to help her? "Why are you with *them*?" she asked, shaking her head.

William scanned the forest behind them. "There was news in Carmathan that you were alive. Thomas and his son Ian had been captured by the Queen. Thomas was there when you escaped—he'd heard you'd gotten out. I was with *them* because they were the only people who knew how to find you."

"She tried to kill me...." Snow White started, her eyes welling up.

She was going to continue, but a twig snapped in the bushes nearby. They turned, seeing the giant warrior who'd tried to shoot her just minutes before. This time the arrow was already in his bow. This time he wouldn't miss.

He raised it, and Snow White turned away, trying to run. But there was thick brush behind her, blocking her path. He let the arrow fly. In an instant, Gus launched himself in front of her, taking the arrow in his chest. He fell to the ground by Snow White's feet, clutching his sides in pain.

The men descended on them. One galloped toward the dwarves with his sword drawn. Duir ducked, the razor-sharp blade clipping off a tuft of his hair. Another launched an arrow at Eric's neck. It missed, instead whizzing by the side of his head. Eric searched the trees, looking for only one face. Then he spotted him. Finn was on horseback, riding through the woods, pursuing Snow White. His greasy hair fell into his eyes. A bruise had formed on his cheek where Eric had struck him.

Eric took off after him, his axes drawn. He would finish what they'd started in the Dark Forest. As long as Finn was alive, Snow White would never be safe. Finn would follow her to Carmathan. He'd wage a war on the duke's castle and burn his land, not satisfied until he had the girl's heart.

He ran through the thick undergrowth. Shadows spread out around him, withering the leaves and grass, shriveling flowers, and sending the fairies scattering into the sky. The creatures of the forest disappeared. The foxes went underground, the turtles burrowed beneath the moss. When he finally stopped running, the woods were completely silent. Finn was nowhere in sight.

He scanned the space between the tree trunks, but it was hard to see anything in the growing darkness. His breath spread out in a cloud before him, the air suddenly much colder than it had been before. Somewhere behind him, a twig snapped. He whipped around, seeing Finn's horse emerge from the woods. He raised his axe, but the horse flew past without a rider.

Eric watched it disappear behind the trees, realizing just a moment too late that it was a trick. He turned as Finn charged out of the woods behind him. Finn brought down his sword, but Eric dodged it, the blade nicking him in the arm. His biceps stung. He glanced down at the wound, which trickled blood onto the shriveled grass below.

Eric didn't hesitate again. He lowered his axe and ran at him. Finn pulled a tree branch back until it was close to snapping, then he let go. The massive limb ricocheted off Eric's chest, sending him flying into a massive oak. The back of his skull met its giant trunk, nearly knocking him out. He could barely move. His breaths were short and painful. The blood streamed down his arm and spread out on his shirt, turning it a deep red.

He watched Finn's face. The weasel smiled, looking so sick and satisfied. He must have loved seeing him like this, his energy drained, a gushing wound in his side. He reached for his axes, but they'd fallen from his waist. They sat on the ground a few feet away.

"I've captured many girls," Finn said, stalking forward. "But your wife was special."

Eric stood up straight, a surge of energy reviving him. "What did you say?" he asked. He eyed the axes in the dirt, knowing he couldn't retrieve them without making himself vulnerable to another strike.

Finn cocked his head to the side. "She fought. When it was clear it was over, she begged. You should know that she called for you. Your Sara."

Eric could barely breathe. A fiery rage ripped through him. Finn was lying—he couldn't have been there. They'd thought it was one of the looters from another village. They'd told him that upon his return. So why was Finn saying differently? Why was he toying with him now?

"How do you know her name?" Eric yelled. He glanced over Finn's shoulder, spotting a fallen tree. Its dead roots stuck up from the ground. The shadows had killed it from the inside out, making the roots dry and sharp. They looked like the pointed wood spears Eric used to hunt with.

"She told me," Finn hissed. "Just before I slit her throat."

That was all Eric needed to hear. He came undone, that day returning to him all at once. Her neck—that beautiful neck he'd held in his hands so many times—had been cut open, the blood crusted black around the wound. He'd run his hands over her dress, feeling the gash in her side, just below her ribs. He kept looking into her face, wondering what kind of monster could hurt a woman like that. What kind of soulless, gutless man could take Sara's life?

Now he knew.

He charged at Finn, not caring about the sword raised in the creep's hand, its blade sharp enough to behead him. He just lowered his shoulder down as he ran, landing a blow in the middle of Finn's abdomen. They went flying into the uprooted tree. Finn landed on its roots with great force, the sharp wooden posts digging into his skin. The bastard howled in agony.

His screams only fueled Eric's anger. *This man killed Sara*, he kept thinking as he pushed Finn's shoulders back, impaling him on the giant tree roots. He didn't stop until they broke through the front of Finn's shirt. Finn writhed in agony, trying to break free of the branches, but Eric held him down.

"Sister!" Finn screamed. He threw his head back. "Heal me, sister!"

The shadows swirled around them. The black smoke curled around the ends of the sharp tree, trying to heal his wounds, but it was impossible. The roots kept them open. Finn bled, the gashes raw around the wood.

Still, the black cloud circled. "Sister?" Finn gasped. Eric never let go of his shoulders. He kept pushing down on him, watching him die, the tears escaping the corners of his eyes. This man had taken his wife. Would he ever be able to love someone as much as he had her?

He'd met Sara one day at the village fair. Tiny rosebuds had been nestled inside her braided bun. She'd been dancing with the others. It was her laugh that he had loved most—that bubbly, buoyant laugh—it'd filled the air, infecting everyone around her.

"You took her," he whispered. He watched as the light left Finn's eyes. "You killed my wife."

When Finn was finally gone, his body limp against the tree roots, Eric turned away. He didn't feel powerful or brave. He wasn't pleased with himself or overjoyed at what he'd done. But there was a quiet consolation in Finn's death. And it wasn't about his own life, for once. Eric thought of Snow White instead.

Maybe Finn's death meant now that Snow White could live free. Maybe she could live in Carmathan in peace.

When he returned to the forest, Finn's men were all dead. The dwarves, fierce warriors themselves, had taken them out one by one. Eric spotted Snow White and the others crowded around someone. As he neared he could see it was Gus, the youngest one. His face was pale. The arrow was still lodged in his chest, right above his heart.

Eric looked around, counting the other dwarves to be certain they were all there. That's when he noticed a young man crouched among them. He couldn't have been more than seventeen. Eric swore he'd recognized him, though he wasn't sure from where.

"Who is this?" he asked.

The boy stood. He puffed out his chest like some silly bird, trying desperately to appear bigger than he was. "My name is William," he said. "I am Duke Hammond's son."

Eric shook his head. *The duke.* The coward who'd been hiding in Carmathan all these years. Of course this was his son. "What is the duke's son doing riding with the Queen's men?" he asked, looking to the dwarves for an answer. Coll and Duir were huddled over Gus, too upset to speak.

William stepped forward. "I was looking for the princess."

"Why?" Eric barked. They had enough trouble as it was. They didn't need some aspiring soldier tagging along with them.

William rested his hand on the butt of his sword. "To protect her."

Eric couldn't help but laugh. "The princess is well protected, as you can see." He gestured around at the seven dwarves, pointing to their crossbows and knives.

William looked Eric up and down. "And who are you?" he challenged.

"The man who got her this far, your *lordship*." He spit the words at him, hating the boy's sense of entitlement. He was a child. Eric stepped forward, getting within inches of his face.

Snow White looked up at him. Her hand was resting on Gus's chest, her face streaked with tears. "Leave him, Huntsman," she said softly. "He's our friend."

Snow White bowed her head, her tears soaking Gus's shirt. Eric stepped back, his face in his hands. The dwarves broke into a funeral chant. Their expressions were tense and sad as they sang. They belted tunes of love and friendship, of life and death. Their songs swelled in the ruined forest. Nothing could warm the air. The animals would not come out from below the earth. The fairies had disappeared. The black cloud that had descended on them still lingered there, circling them in dark, curling wisps.

When the song ended, Coll and Duir brought armfuls of wood to burn in the funeral pyre. Quert laid stones on the ground in a giant rectangle, making a bed for Gus to sleep on. They moved his tiny body, stacking the dead branches on top of him, crisscrossing each one until he disappeared beneath the wood. Beith worked at a piece of flint, finally lighting it.

They stood there together, watching as it burned. The flames grew. The logs popped and crackled as they were engulfed. Some of the dwarves cried. Who, Eric did not know. All he could hear were Snow White's sobs, her sadness enough to send shivers down his spine. He kept staring at the side of her face, wishing he could take her pain from her. But as night fell, their sorrow only grew. This was not the end of their battle—this was the beginning.

For their twisted, evil Queen was still alive.

avenna lay in bed, studying the back of her hand. It had returned to normal, the brown age spots gone, the horrible puckered skin now so smooth and taut. She rested her delicate fingers on her sternum, trying to slow her breaths. A full hour had gone by since Finn had passed on. This was the longest it had ever taken for her to feel young again.

Two girls. Not one—two. She had consumed both quickly and hungrily, sucking the energy from their tiny, sweet mouths, feeling it fill her from the tips of her toes to the top of her head. Her strength had returned. But even their beauty, the softness of their hair or their creamy, porcelain skin, wasn't enough. The grief still ripped through her. An emptiness had filled the space beneath her ribs. She felt as if someone had scooped out her insides.

Her only brother. What had she meant to him, and he to her? They had been the only two left who remembered that day at the camp when the king's troops had swarmed the wagons. They'd played together in the forest, darting behind the trees, hiding from each other. Finn was the only other person who'd known their mother's face.

She'd been in the bath when she heard his first scream. She was below the surface of the milk, letting the smooth liquid cover every inch of her skin, softening it. His shrill cry echoed inside her, as if he were right there in the room with her. She twisted and turned, feeling the sharp tree roots bury themselves in her back. The Huntsman gripped her shoulders as he had gripped Finn's, pushing her back into the wooden knives. She felt the soft tissue inside her chest tearing. The pain ripped through her, so strong her toes curled under and her hands balled into tight little fists.

She tried so hard. She summoned all the power her mother had given her and channeled it through Finn, trying to give him the strength to fight. When that didn't work, she tried to close his wounds. But with the tree roots in his flesh, it was no use. Slowly, with each passing second, she grew weaker. Her body aged. Her hair went white. The skin on her face turned wrinkled and loose.

"Forgive me, brother," she'd finally whispered when it seemed the wounds would take both their lives. She had to cut their connection. She couldn't fight anymore.

She'd drummed her fingers on her breastbone, knowing what had to be done. She was alone. No one besides her own brother would hunt the girl, following her into the Dark Forest and beyond, fighting the Huntsman and those nasty dwarves in the process. Now, if she still wanted the girl's heart, she would have to retrieve it herself....

She stood, a quiet incantation forming on her lips. She spoke so low the words were barely audible, instead coming out as a low, uneven hum. Outside the castle, the birds cried in the trees. The first raven swooped down and landed, with a bloody thud, against the window's thin pane. A tiny crack spread out around where the bird had hit it, weakening the glass.

Within seconds, another bird appeared from the trees. It slammed into the same window, its beak breaking on impact. One bird, then another, darted down, until the glass shattered, the shards scattering across the stone floor. The first birds of the flock came inside the throne room. They flew around the great curve of the walls, circling Ravenna in a giant swarm. More came out of the trees and through the broken window, until she disappeared beneath them. Her arms were raised, and her head was back. Had anyone been able to see her in the horrible black mass of feathers, they would have known she was smiling.

A day passed, and no one spoke Gus's name. They'd covered miles of barren hills, crossed shallow streams, and trudged through dead flowerbeds, the dwarves leading in front, the Huntsman and William trailing behind. The sun was setting as they reached the base of the rugged mountains. The duke's stronghold was in the valley beyond them. It couldn't be more than two days' walk.

Snow White followed behind Coll and Duir. She kept her eyes on the ground, unable to believe what had happened. She remembered Gus's face as he'd lain there in the withered leaves. His breaths had gotten raspy and short until they slowly stopped. He had sacrificed himself so she could live. Now, in the aftermath, she wished he hadn't. She wished she had been the one to take that arrow. The guilt was too much. These last hours, she'd wondered what the other men thought. Did they blame her? Did they secretly wish they'd never stumbled upon her that day in the woods?

She wiped her eyes, trying to get the image of Gus out of her head. It took her a minute to realize that William had fallen in line beside her. He stared at her, his face full of concern.

"What?" Snow White asked, sensing something was wrong.

William glanced back at the Huntsman, gauging how far away he was. "I'm sorry," he said, his voice nearly a whisper. "I'm so sorry I left you." He rubbed his forehead, his eyes misting over.

"You didn't," Snow White tried. She reached for his hand.

William shook his head. "If I'd have known you were alive, I would have come sooner."

The dwarves started into the woods. Coll and Duir dropped their satchels down behind some rocks. The others followed, setting up camp. Snow White paused at the edge of the forest and looked into William's hazel eyes. Never once, in all the years in that tower, had she ever blamed him for what happened. When the loneliness had nearly driven her mad, when she couldn't take the bugs that climbed the walls or the sound of explosions in the distance, she had thought of him. He had been there with her. Those memories were the only thing that had kept her alive.

"We were children, William," she said. "You're here now." She squeezed his hand.

She looked into the camp. The dwarves were dragging fallen branches and old twigs into a pile. They worked quietly, not meeting one another's eyes, the sadness of the day still upon them. She walked toward them, gesturing for William to follow. It was no good to look back, to apologize for what had happened, or to wonder what could have been different. Who could say what either of them *should* have done? She'd been torturing herself thinking of the attack yesterday. What use was that? All she felt was a hard, painful knot in the pit of her stomach.

She knelt down beside William, pulling up dried moss to use as kindling. He did the same, working quietly with his hands, his face softer than before. Snow White looked back at the darkening sky. Ravens circled overhead. They still had another day or two until they reached Carmathan, and Ravenna would come for them soon. They had to look forward and ahead.

Snow White sat on the edge of the camp, listening to the chorus of snores behind her. The dwarves had fallen asleep quickly, as had William and the Huntsman. But hours later, Snow White was still awake, an uneasy feeling spreading through her. She scanned the forest around them. The sun was just coming up on the horizon, filling the sky with a strange orange glow. Did Ravenna already know Finn was dead? Could she sense it? Snow White thought again of Rose in her cell. Her face had been wrinkled and spotted with age, her shoulders bent forward. Ravenna had powers no one else did. How long would it be until the Queen found her?

Leaves rustled behind her. She straightened up, feeling for the knife at her belt. She wrapped her fingers around the end of it and spun around, pointing the blade in front of her. William stood before her. His brown hair was messy from sleep.

"It's only me," he said. He held up both hands until she

lowered the knife, slipping it back at her side. "Come. Walk with me." He started away from the camp, making sure the Huntsman was out of earshot. He tried to pat his hair down as they walked.

Soon they were deep in the forest, completely alone. The silver birches rose up around them. A light dusting of snow covered the earth. "Up here, it's as if nothing has changed. The world looks beautiful again," she said, shaking her head. Her voice was calmer now that William was by her side. She felt just a little less alone.

"It will be. When you are queen," he said. Snow White turned to him, unsure why he'd say that. Why was everyone so certain they could defeat Ravenna's army? Had they not seen her magic? "The people of this kingdom hate Ravenna with their very fiber," he explained.

She shook her head. She remembered what Ravenna had said the day of her wedding—how they were bound together. "It's strange...." Snow White started. "But I feel only sorrow for her."

William cocked his head to one side, curious. "Once people find out you're alive, they will rise up in your name. You are the king's daughter, and the rightful heir."

"How am I supposed to do this? How do I inspire?" Snow White said, shaking her head. "How do I lead men?" Gus was dead because of her. She had asked the dwarves to take her to Carmathan. How could she be responsible for many more lives when she had failed one man already?

William smiled. "The same way you led me when we were

children. I followed you everywhere, ran when you called. I would've done anything for you." He stared at her intently.

She turned away, feeling the heat rise in her cheeks. "That's not how I remember it." Wasn't she the one who'd followed William up the apple tree that day? He was always teasing her, telling her to run faster, complaining that she wasn't a boy. He wanted someone to dig up rocks with and chase through the castle courtyard. "I remember we were always arguing. And fighting, and..." She would have gone on, but he was looking at her so intensely, his eyes searching her face for something unseen.

He leaned so close, she could feel his breath on her skin. He smiled, his cheeks flushed. His lips were just inches from hers. Then he pulled something from his pocket and held it between them. Snow White looked down at the apple. Its white-and-red skin didn't have a mark on it. William inched it toward her, a mischievous grin crossing his lips.

"I know this trick." Snow White laughed, remembering it from all those years before.

"What trick?" William asked. He held it up, just inches from her face, daring her to take it from him.

Snow White smiled. After all these years, he remembered. She wondered if he'd thought of her as often as she'd thought of him. Maybe, in some ways, those memories had kept him alive, too. She snatched it from his hands. Before he could retrieve it, she bit into the thin skin, letting the sweet juices run down her throat.

William's eyes narrowed. There was something strange

in his smile. He looked on, watching her chew, laughing as she swallowed. She felt a strong pain in her chest. Something was terribly wrong. As she gasped for breath, William looked on, his face more familiar than it ever had been before. She stumbled and fell, collapsing in the snow.

Her limbs went numb. She stared up at the sky, trying to move her fingers or toes. It was useless. Her body felt like it was made of lead. She couldn't even blink. William's face appeared in view, his hair falling down over his eyes, which now glowed a brilliant blue. She realized at once it wasn't William at all—it was *her*. Ravenna had found her after all.

"You see, child," Ravenna said. William's face changed, revealing the full lips Snow White had admired as a child, and Ravenna's small, delicate nose. "By fairest blood it was done, and only by fairest blood can it be undone. You were the only one who could break the spell and end my life, and the only one pure enough to save me."

Snow White's heart pounded in her ears. Ravenna's clothes changed back. She wore a black cloak covered with raven feathers that rustled around her high cheekbones in a tall collar. She reached into it, retrieving a jeweled dagger. Then she ran it along Snow White's breast bone, marking the spot where her heart was. Snow White opened her mouth to scream, but nothing came out.

Ravenna leaned down. She pressed her lips to Snow White's ear. "You don't realize how lucky you are. You'll never know what it is to grow old."

Off in the distance, Snow White heard the crunching sound

of footsteps in the snow. Ravenna looked up, alarmed. She raised the dagger above Snow White's chest, about to drive it through her sternum, but then she instantly transformed into a dense mass of ravens. The sky above Snow White was filled with them. The black birds circled in one great swarm, flying around her body. Bloody feathers fell to the ground. A few cawed loudly. Others took off through the trees. Snow White could see the Huntsman's bloody axes swiping through the mass.

William appeared, cutting at the birds with his sword. Their dead bodies fell into the snow around her. The dwarves came running as well, hearing the cries from Eric and William. The men kept swinging at the air until all the wretched creatures were gone. Snow White's vision blurred, and her eyelashes fluttered. She heard them calling to her, but their voices seemed farther away now, the words running together in a strange, low hum.

William knelt down beside her. He cradled her head in his hands. She couldn't feel his fingers on her skin. His mouth was moving, but there were no words coming out. She fixed her gaze on his face, watching as it changed, overcome with sorrow.

He kissed her. She couldn't even feel his lips on her own. It was as if he were kissing someone else as she watched from far away. He pulled back, and his lips formed her name, calling again, and he crushed his mouth again to hers. But it had no effect.

She left the world just as fast as she came into it, and the scene before her went black.

ric stood in the doorway of the cold tomb, a flask in his hand. It was strange to see the girl like this, so silent and still, her arms folded over her chest. She lay on the stone block as though she were just resting there for the evening, enjoying a long slumber. If it weren't for her pale face and cold purple lips, he would've never known she was dead.

So he'd gotten her here after all. He had kept his promise, almost despite himself, and had taken her to the duke's castle. He'd never imagined coming here like this, though. They'd carried her through the snow to the stronghold, finally delivering her to the duke. The boy, William, had explained to his father what had happened. Ravenna had taken her from them. Somehow she'd gotten past them in the night. She'd come into their camp, where they slept, and killed her. Somehow they hadn't noticed her presence until it was too late.

Eric took another swig of the grog, enjoying the familiar burning in his throat. He'd watched the mourners file into the duke's castle. Mothers had brought their children to see her. The princess they had believed was dead had been taken from them once again. A few grown men had walked past her, tears in their eyes. They'd knelt before her body and prayed. She represented something to them—he could tell that by all the grief they felt. They hadn't known the king's daughter, had never seen her smile and hadn't enjoyed the fierce look she got in her eyes if you dared challenge her. But this was still an end for them, too.

The duke had spoken to his son, telling him they would not retaliate. There would be no war in Snow White's honor. He was a coward—just as Eric had always thought. How many more people had to die by the Queen's hand before he would strike back? What was the point of an army, however small, if not to fight?

Eric stepped toward the girl, drinking down the last of the alcohol, wishing it numbed him more. "Here you are," he said, his voice echoing in the cold chamber. "Where it ends. Dressed up too pretty." He stood over her, noticing the stiffness in her fingers. It was almost too much to see her this way, just as Sara had been. So drained of everything real. Snow White had been right beside him as he went to sleep. He'd watched as she rested against the rock, lost in thought, her hands combing through her tangled hair. He had seen her just before he drifted off.

How had he not heard Ravenna? And why hadn't she

come for him first, the man who killed her brother? He hated himself for letting it happen. He'd awoken with a start, sensing something was wrong. He'd taken off into the woods. He'd flown through the silver birches, seeing Ravenna hovering over her. She'd changed shape as soon as he'd struck her with his axe.

"You're asleep," he tried desperately, taking another swig from the flask. "About to wake up and give me more grief. Am I right?"

He reached out, his hand hovering just above hers, not certain he could do it. Slowly, he set his palm down, feeling how cold she was. He pinched the end of her sleeve, taking in the beaded pink dress they had put her in. It was so frilly and feminine. He somehow knew she would've hated it.

He swallowed hard. She wouldn't want him to turn into some bumbling mess—not over this. Not over her. "You deserved better," he said softly. He studied her face. Her black hair had been done in curls. Someone had placed a rose behind her ear, though it was wilting now.

"She was my wife," he said, speaking as though she were alive. The words came easier with the grog. "That was your question that went unanswered. Sara was her name. When I came back from the wars, I carried with me the stench of death and the anger of the lost. I wasn't worth saving, but she did so anyway. I loved her more than anything or anyone. I let her out of my sight, and she was gone."

He lowered his head. "I became myself again. And it was a self I never cared for. Until you. You remind me of her.

Her spirit, her heart. And now you are gone, too." He faltered over his words, feeling the knot rise in the back of his throat. "You both deserved better. And I'm sorry to have failed you as well."

The torchlight cast a warm glow on her face. He reached down, brushing a strand of hair off her forehead. "You will be queen in heaven now." He leaned down and pressed his lips to hers, just for a moment, the gesture calming him. Then he turned away, throwing the flask on the ground. Yes, he was drinking again. He was certain she would've hated that, too.

He left the stone chamber, his footsteps echoing off the walls. The Huntsman never looked back. Had he turned and studied her, he might've seen the faint color returning to her cheeks, or the way her eyelids fluttered. Snow White's lips parted ever so slightly. Then she drew in her first breath, the tiny gasp barely audible in the giant tomb.

Fric reached the gate just after sunrise. His head throbbed from the night before. The old pains had returned. The blood pulsed in his stitched-up wounds. "Open the gate!" he yelled to the soldiers stationed above. He was careful not to look directly at them, afraid he'd be recognized. "Open the gate!" he yelled again, but it didn't move. He glanced up. The men were looking past him, at the beaten path to the castle. A young man was coming after him. He walked slowly, struggling with the burlap sack in his hand.

"Huntsman!" the young man called. Eric lowered his head. He had been so careful at the procession. He kept his eyes down, his hair covering the sides of his face, trying to go unnoticed. He'd been there less than twelve hours—how did they realize it was him?

The young man ran toward him. He wore a white linen shirt and clean trousers, his black hair oiled to the side. Eric recognized him as one of the duke's clerks. Percy . . . was that his name? "Yes, I recognized you." Percy nodded, as if in apology.

Eric sighed. He held up his hands in front of him. "Look, if you want—"

"We have no quarrel with you," the young man said. "Not anymore. You returned the princess to us. For that . . ." He hoisted the sack into Eric's arms. Eric cradled it, suddenly realizing what it was.

The gold coins were heavier than he'd imagined they'd be. He had already spent the money in his mind—on a house in the countryside, beyond the kingdom, on the horse that would get him there. When he was traveling through the Dark Forest, in those hours after he'd met the girl, he'd bought three new axes, a fur-lined winter coat, and cowhide boots. He'd actually counted the flagons he could trade for with just one of these coins (two hundred and thirty-three).

But now that they were right here, in his arms, he didn't want them anymore. He'd failed her in the worst way of all. Who could care about coins when Snow White was dead? He passed it back to the young man. "Keep your money," he said, turning to go.

He didn't get more than a few feet before stopping. Inside the castle walls, he heard the roar of applause. There were shouts and cheers. He looked at the young man for an explanation, but Percy just shrugged. Eric couldn't see beyond the castle's stone facade. But he started back in anyway, sensing already that something had changed. He quickened his pace as the cheers rose up around him, even louder than before.

Snow White stood at the top of the stairs, overlooking the castle courtyard. The duke's men had set up canvas tents in the open air for all the kingdom's refugees. Families huddled beside fires for warmth; others stood on the twisting soup line, waiting for their breakfast. Muir and Quert sat beside each other. They spoke quietly outside a battered tent, blankets draped over their shoulders.

She'd awoken suddenly, the Huntsman's voice echoing in the stone chamber. She'd noticed the torches beside the funeral bier. The walls were covered with a thin layer of grime. Little by little, she could smell the mildew in the air. She heard the condensation dripping from the ceiling to the floor. That sound counted out the passing minutes. Within the hour, the feeling in her legs returned.

As she slowly came back to herself, her mind awake inside her still body, she thought only of Ravenna. She'd pressed her lips against Snow White's ear. "You were the only one who could break the spell and end my life," she'd said. "You were the only one." As Snow White breathed again, the warmth returning to her hands, it was so clear. There was only one thing left to do.

She started down the stairs. Quert saw her first. He whispered to Muir, who called to the other dwarves. They came outside the tent, staring up at her, their eyes wide. "It's a miracle!" Beith shouted across the courtyard. He pointed to her as she came down the last steps.

William and Duke Hammond looked on in awe. Women and children left their tents and huddled at the base of the stairs. William covered his mouth, unable to speak.

"Your Highness..." Duke Hammond said. He covered her hands with his and searched her face. He was so much older than she'd remembered him. His hair had gone completely white. He was bent forward with age. "We thought you..."

William came forward, resting his hand on her shoulder, as if to affirm that she was real. Snow White shook her head. She couldn't say what had awoken her from her sleep. In those hours, she'd heard nothing and felt nothing. The last thing she remembered was the black birds circling above her head and the glinting blade of the axe, sending them scattering into the sky. All she knew was that she was alive now, here, and there was something she had to do.

"No, my lord," she said softly.

The people in the courtyard all looked on. Far off, near the back tents, the Huntsman stood, shaking his head in disbelief. He walked toward her until he was close enough that she could see his face. Tears filled his eyes.

Duke Hammond gestured to a wooden chair. "You must rest—"

"I have rested long enough," she said. She looked out on the thick crowd. A woman was crying, her face in her hands as she told her children how Snow White had been brought back from the dead. "It's a miracle," everyone kept whispering. That word hung the air.

Snow White looked into the duke's gray eyes. His face was covered in wrinkles. "I am ready to ride by your side, my lord," she said, "when you face the Queen in battle."

William stared at the dirt. The duke looked down at his hands on hers, his face full of concern. "There will be no battle, Your Highness. The best thing you can do for your people is stay safe behind these walls."

Snow White looked at the emaciated children behind him. They looked at her with the same sad, desperate eyes she'd seen in the ruined village. "That is all I thought to do when I escaped. But I have come to learn there is no peace while others suffer."

The duke squeezed her hands. "The Queen cannot be defeated," he said loudly. The soldiers around him nodded. "She cannot be killed. There can be no victory."

Snow White turned to the group of generals behind him, remembering Ravenna's words. "I can defeat her. I am the only one—she told me so herself."

She pulled away from Duke Hammond and started into the courtyard to address the hundreds of refugees who'd gathered around them. Soldiers looked on, clutching their helmets in their hands. The dwarves held their hats over their hearts.

"I have been told that I represent you," Snow White called out, the words coming easily. She felt nothing but peace. Never had she been so certain of anything. "I have

193

been told my place is not to fight but to stay here, safely behind these walls. I will not." She looked at Muir, who was staring in her direction, his eyes glittering.

"I hold life sacred, even more since I've tasted freedom," Snow White continued. "But I've lost my fear of death. If Ravenna comes for me, I will ride to meet her. And if she doesn't come for me, I will ride to meet her. Alone, if I must." Snow White turned to the generals standing outside a massive tent. "But if you join me, I will gladly give my life for you. Because this land and its people have lost too much."

Her heart pounded in her chest. She stood before them, her shoulders back, waiting for their support. Duke Hammond studied her carefully, taking in her pale pink funeral robes and the hair that cascaded down her back. She waited, listening to the sound of the birds crying out in the distance. She wondered if she would have to leave tonight on horseback, alone, and face Ravenna herself. Then, slowly, the duke bowed his head in reverence. William got down on one knee, following his father's lead. The knights and generals followed.

She met the Huntsman's gaze. There was a tenderness in his eyes as he smiled, then bowed down before her. The dwarves followed. Soon the entire courtyard was kneeling, showing their respect. She was their leader, just as her father had been. She swore she would end Ravenna's reign, or lose her life trying.

Snow White stood before them, tears welling in her

eyes. She could almost feel their victory already—it seemed so close. She imagined the kingdom again, as it had been under her father's rule. She saw the green pastures and the village fairs, the children dancing around the maypole. The fields would be fruitful again, the farms sending out full carts every day in every direction. No one would go hungry. And every child would be safe.

There was only one more thing to say now that they were here, waiting to fight. They had shown the courage she knew they'd always possessed.

"Then it is done," she announced, signaling for the people—*her* people—to rise. "We will leave tonight."

Snow White rode out in front. The chain mail was heavy on her back, its cold metal stinging her skin. She held her shield by her side, enjoying how natural it felt on her arm. It was just like the one her father had ridden with. Their family crest was inlaid on the front. She remembered how he had shown it to her as a child, letting her trace her fingers over the gold branches of the oak tree. Its roots sunk into the earth. The top of the trunk was pointed in a cross, just like the crown. "It's a symbol of strength," he'd said, showing her the roots. "It's held so firmly in place, connected to the earth by all that's unseen. It grows tall and proud."

She held it out, comforted by the weight of it. She felt him now as she listened to the steady hoofbeats behind her. Her father was everywhere she looked—in the crescent moon, the shifting trees and crashing waves. As they crested the hill by the beach, less than ten miles from Ravenna's castle, she could nearly feel him by her side.

She turned back, looking to the duke, William, and Eric, who rode behind her. There were hundreds of men and women following them, their faces glowing in the torchlight. The army—*her* army—extended well into the woods. She was taken aback by the bravery of those who had volunteered. Boys no older than fifteen. Mothers and fathers, peasants and rebels. Some had been at Carmathan, surviving all these years at the duke's stronghold, and still others had come out of hiding in the woods, taking their meager supplies and joining the fight. With every mile they covered, their army grew. Now she stood on the hill above the beach, looking out on Ravenna's castle, a few hundred soldiers behind her.

As Snow White and the duke pulled out front, a general rode up beside them. "My lord," he said, pointing down at the rocky shore, "we only have an hour or two before the tide comes in. Not long enough to breach the castle walls. We'll either be completely exposed or drowned by the ocean."

The duke shook his head. "Is there any other way in? Tunnels? Caves?"

Snow White didn't bother looking at them. She kept her eyes on the black ocean, at the very spot where she'd emerged the week before. The tide was still low. Rocks jutted out from underneath the waves. She noticed the opening in the side of the cliff's ledge—the same sewer she'd crawled out of.

She shifted her eyes to the beach below. The dwarves had already reached the water's edge and were wading in. They crouched low in the shallows, just as she had directed them to. It wouldn't take them longer than an hour to reach the sewer entrance. They were already halfway there. "If we are at the portcullis when the sun clears the horizon, it will be open," she said firmly, guiding her horse down the rocky hill. She turned back, staring into the duke's and the general's nervous faces. William and Eric followed her without question, and the entire army spread out along the beach.

They moved down the beach, passing the stone labyrinth Snow White had stumbled into when she came ashore. As the tide rose, the horses and soldiers were pushed up onto the sand. They kept moving as the waves came ever closer, threatening to pin them against the steep rock ledge. "We don't have much time," Duke Hammond said.

Snow White stared out at the ocean. She could see the dwarves ducking under each wave. They were nearly at the sewer entrance. The sun was almost at the horizon. As soon as it came up, the riders would be visible on the beach, and they'd lose any chance of a surprise attack. They had to charge and hope the portcullis was up in time. It was their only choice. "We should ride now," Snow White said, turning to the duke. "They'll have the portcullis up by the time we arrive."

As the duke raised his sword, ordering the soldiers forward, Snow White turned back to Eric. He was just behind William and the generals—they'd insisted the military be out front. She met his gaze for only a moment, but he seemed to sense what she wanted. He rode up beside her, breaking rank, and their horses sped up. Riding together, the salt air stinging her eyes, she felt no fear.

They rode forward, the army speeding up, their eyes on the cliff ledge, where the castle was. Slowly it came into view. Snow White's heart sped up. The portcullis was still down. The black grate could be seen even from half a mile away. The duke turned to her, his face full of concern, but she didn't slow down. Coll and Duir—all of them should've been in the castle courtyard already. Any minute now, the gate would go up.

She glanced over her shoulder, looking at the massive army on the beach. The tide came up around them, the horses splashing in the waves as they rode forward. The sun had come up, warming the sky. They were completely exposed. "Come on," Snow White whispered to herself, willing the portcullis to open. "Hurry..."

But then she noticed the tiny flickering lights along the top of the castle wall. The trebuchets were being loaded. The pinpoints of light rose up in the air, and the fiery missiles rained down on them. A fireball exploded just a few feet beside her. But Snow White didn't stop. She kept her head down, riding faster toward the castle walls.

The army faltered. Some of the troops stalled when they saw the flaming missiles coming at them. One man fell from his horse as the ground blew up beneath him. There was no choice now. If they didn't keep going to the castle walls, they'd be drowned by the rising tide. It was rushing in, the ocean flooding over the sand, coming up around the horse's legs. Snow White held up her shield, urging the soldiers on.

There were screams behind her. She turned, seeing a blond woman who'd been hit by a flaming arrow. The horse whinnied, throwing her off. Her body was trampled as the other soldiers rode on. Snow White swallowed hard, steeling herself against the gore. Two generals fell beside her. One was struck in the neck with an arrow. All around her, there was blood and fire. Every few seconds, she glanced sideways at the Huntsman, thankful that he was still there.

Smoke filled the air. The wind shifted, and she spotted the castle entrance again. The portcullis was still down. She rode at the wall, knowing that they only had a few more minutes. Ten, at most. If it wasn't up by the time they arrived, they'd be trapped there against the rocks. Ravenna's soldiers would be above them, the ocean rushing in from the side.

More archers appeared at the castle wall. Snow White held her shield above her head as she rode to protect herself. She heard the arrows hit off the top of it. She could feel their heat against her arm. She didn't look back. Someone was yelling for help. Bodies floated facedown in the surf. A spotted gray horse had fallen on the rocks. It was crying out, a blistering wound in its side. It writhed in pain as the salt water washed over it. She desperately wished someone would end its life.

William rode out in front of her, his shield above him. "You must turn back!" he yelled. She could barely hear him over the sound of the waves.

"I gave my word I would stand with them!" Snow White called to him. A rider beside her was struck in the shoulder with a flaming arrow. He tried to pull it from his chest, but it was too late. His clothes had caught fire. He twisted and fell into the waves, crying out in pain.

Snow White started up the incline toward the castle, not heeding William's warning. They didn't have a choice anymore. The only way to save themselves was to fight. She rode toward the massive iron gate at full speed. Any second, it would come up. Any second, the dwarves would raise it. Flaming arrows rained down all around her as she neared. She kept her shield up, hoping she wasn't wrong.

When she was only fifty feet away, the giant gate came up. She could just make out Gort and Nion clinging to the ends of the rope, using their bodies as a counterweight. William and Eric rode on either side of her as they galloped under the gate into the castle courtyard, the army right behind them.

The archers high above spun around, aiming at the soldiers who'd made it inside. As more of the army got past the portcullis, they outnumbered Ravenna's guards three to one.

"Line up!" Snow White called to Eric and William. If they made a wedge formation, spreading out across the courtyard on a diagonal, they could corner Ravenna's guards. The fight would be over within minutes.

A few generals stormed ahead, forming the front line. Snow White, William, and Eric kept their shields up at an angle, staying right behind them. The flaming arrows fell against their shields. Eric burst out front, taking out two guards with his hatchets. William drove his sword into another guard's side. Snow White rammed another man with her shield, pinning him against the courtyard wall. His head hit the stone, and he fell to the ground, unconscious.

There were only a handful of guards remaining. A few of Snow White's army hooted loudly, already sensing that the fight was over. Four of Ravenna's guards turned and ran for safety through the castle corridors. The ones who were left set their weapons on the ground in surrender.

Snow White turned back, searching the men for signs of the duke. He was just a few people behind her in the dense formation. Their eyes met, and he smiled, a look of relief on his face. It was over—they both knew it now. They just had to find Ravenna. Whatever magic she had, Snow White could overcome. The Queen had said so herself.

Then something in the duke's face changed. He furrowed his brows. He looked past Snow White, up into the courtyard rafters. She followed his gaze, studying the strange black shadows that huddled there beneath the eaves. The army quieted. Eric pointed to an arched doorway where a black shadow hung in the air. They watched it. Slowly, the shadows condensed into figures. Dark warriors emerged from every archway and every corridor. Snow White glanced around, her shield slippery in her hand as she realized the truth: They were surrounded on all sides.

The shadow soldiers swarmed them. One charged
Eric. The Huntsman slashed through his chest
with the hatchet. The man shattered like glass,
the tiny splintered shards exploding from his center.
Within seconds, the man reformed, the pieces coming back
together. He charged Eric again, swinging his glinting sword.

Snow White had never seen anything like it. All around
her, the shadow warriors were attacking her army. Men fell,
unable to keep up with the vicious blows, which came one
after the next. The shadows showed no signs of tiring. Their
faces were strange and featureless. Every wound they endured
quickly healed. As they moved, driving their swords into her
army, she felt someone's eyes on her. She glanced up at the
third-floor balcony. There, Ravenna stood, her black-
feathered cloak wrapped tightly around her. She smiled as
her eyes shifted to the magic army, the dark warriors finish-
ing their attack.

Snow White didn't hesitate. In the corner, by the stair-well, bodies were piled up. Resistant to pain, the shadow warriors were killing quickly. They speared one of her soldiers with their swords, then turned on another. She raced at one of the shadows, blocking it with her shield. The dark warrior stumbled back, giving her enough time to run. She swung her sword at another and shattered it. She kept weaving through the courtyard, the battle surging around her, when she finally reached the stairs. She darted up into the silent corridors, startled by the sound of her own panting breath.

She pulled out her sword as she made her way up the second flight. It was the same wing of the castle that her father had lived in all those years before. It was different now, though. The curtains were tattered. The long hallway was dark, with no torches to light the way. A dresser was toppled on its side, the wood buckling from the mildew.

Beside her, a door stood ajar, the room glowing with an eerie light. She turned, taking in the Queen's throne room. A jeweled chair sat against the wall. Polished swords hung above it. There was a wooden case filled with ornate crowns and massive rubies. Snow White held her sword in front of her, taking it all in. Through another doorway, standing off to the side before a massive bronze mirror, was Ravenna. Snow White met her eyes in the warped reflection.

"It ends today," Snow White said, stalking forward. "I've come for you."

Ravenna turned, a slight smirk on her lips. "So my rose

has returned," she said, laughing. She looked down at Snow White's sword. "With a thorn. Come, avenge the father who was too weak to raise his sword." She pulled her jeweled dagger from her cloak, spinning it in her hand.

Snow White climbed the low steps and stood before Ravenna, looking into her piercing blue eyes. The anger rose in her chest. How dare Ravenna speak of her father—the very man she'd murdered?

"For my father," Snow White said, holding her sword aloft. "For the kingdom and for me." She lunged at Ravenna, but the Queen darted away. She slunk back, circling Snow White from behind. Snow White turned and slashed at her again. Ravenna moved too quickly, though, and stepped to the other side of the chamber.

Footsteps sounded in the stone corridor. Snow White turned to see Eric and William in the entrance of the throne room. Ravenna raised her arm. With one flick of her finger, the ceiling above them shattered. The glass shards fell, the gray pieces re-forming into dark fairies. They swarmed the men, cutting them off from Snow White.

When Ravenna was satisfied that they wouldn't be disturbed, she turned back to the girl, her blue eyes studying her. This child—the one she had saved so many years ago—was now coming back to kill her. The irony of it all was almost too much. Ravenna hadn't wanted the girl to die, but there was no choice. The mirror had said so—it was her life or Snow White's. And she'd gone on entertaining this feud long enough.

Snow White charged her, sword drawn. When she was just a foot away, Ravenna turned and tripped her, sending the girl facedown on the floor. Her pathetic sword careened across the room, to the far side of the mirror chamber. Ravenna hovered over her, her eyes fixed on Snow White's breast bone. He heart was so close—in minutes, she would hold it in her hand. This time, she would not be stopped.

"This is all life has to offer," Ravenna cooed. She stared into Snow White's massive brown eyes, almost feeling a little sorry for the girl. "Time passes. Hope dies. But all is not lost. For at least now, one of us will live forever...." Ravenna raised her jeweled dagger as she had done ten years before, the night of her wedding. It was just as easy now as it was then. She let out a breath, bringing it down toward Snow White's chest, when the girl blocked her with her forearm and twisted her wrist. Pain ripped through Ravenna's chest, and she let out a scream, shaking from the impact.

She looked down to the tender space where her ribs met in the center. The girl had driven a knife into her. Ravenna gasped, but she could feel the blood in her lungs. She felt like she was drowning. It was impossible to get air.

Ravenna fell to the ground, the stone floor cold against her back. "A life for a life. By fairest blood, it is undone," she whispered.

"Hope never dies," Snow White whispered back. The girl knelt beside the Queen, cradling her head in her hands, as Ravenna tried desperately to breathe. It was no use. Blood ran down her chest, pooling on the floor. Her vision blurred. This wasn't how it was supposed to happen. But a tiny part of her supposed it was only right—the girl was only doing what Ravenna herself had done years earlier, avenging her family.

From where she lay, Ravenna could see the dark fairies in the throne room disappear. As they changed into tiny clouds of smoke, she knew it was over. She was dying, the last of her magic powers gone.

23

After Ravenna slipped away, her body still warm to the touch, Snow White finally let go of her hand. She walked past the Huntsman and William, down through the corridor, and out onto the balcony. The shadow warriors had vanished. Bodies were strewn all over the courtyard. Swords and shields were scattered about, blood smeared across their fronts. Soldiers lay in twisted heaps. A few of the injured staggered out of the portcullis, looking for help. The destruction was great. But Snow White gazed beyond it, noticing a patch of light in the cloister garden.

Though it was spring, the branches were withered and brown. They held not a single blossom. During the battle, a dark shadow had consumed everything around the castle. But now it lifted, ever so slowly. The colors of the kingdom were more vivid than Snow White had seen them in years. Leaves burst from the tree branches. A flock of magpies darted past, their blue wings catching the sunlight. All around her, there were signs of life stirring. The duke staggered out of a corridor below, a beautiful young woman following him.

She looked up, her gaze meeting Snow White's. She was even more radiant than she had been before, her pale, round face young again. Rose waved, the smile calming Snow White's racing heart. Snow White waved back, wiping the tears from her eyes.

The following day, she sat before the kingdom in the same cathedral she'd been in ten years before. She stared out at the full pews, taking in the dwarves, who were crammed side by side in one row. Their faces were clean-shaven, their hair oiled back and parted at the side. Duke Hammond had ordered them specially tailored suits for the occasion. Snow White nearly laughed as she watched them shift in their seats, obviously uncomfortable by such formal attire.

"Are you ready, my Queen?" William asked. They stood side by side, their shoulders nearly touching. He reached out for her hand and gave it one subtle squeeze.

She glanced sideways at him and smiled, knowing it would be easier if she felt what the entire kingdom wanted her to feel for him. They loved this young man, the rebel leader, Duke Hammond's son. But in her mind, he still remained the boy she'd grown up with, the one who'd teased her in the apple tree. He was William—always and forever, her good friend.

Duke Hammond set the crown on her head. Weighed down by the rubies and sapphires, it was heavier than she'd imagined it would be. Anna and Lily stood in the second row, raising their hands in applause. The room broke out into cheers.

But out of all the now familiar faces in the great hall, Snow White kept returning to one. The Huntsman stood at the back entrance. He'd worn a similar outfit the day they'd met, but now his linen shirt was neatly pressed. His pants weren't stained with grog. His shaggy hair was tucked behind his ears. If she hadn't known him better, she would've said he looked handsome.

He had already told her he was leaving, that there was no place for him here in the castle among royalty. *Royalty*—he'd always said that word with such disdain. There was no arguing with him when he got like that. No telling him what to do and why. Maybe she was his Queen now, but Eric still lived by different rules. And the more she knew him, the more she wondered if that one inescapable rule of his would ever change. *Would he always be alone?*

He brought his hand on his forehead, nodding as he left. She watched him go. She had seen a kingdom fall, the deaths of so many men and women. Explosions and fire had surrounded her. She'd faced death and returned. Why, then, did she feel such sorrow now, the sadness so great it brought tears to her eyes? He was just one man.

She was relieved when Beith cried out, splitting the

silence in the cathedral. "All hail the Queen!" he yelled. Then the others joined in, their voices rising up around her.

She was no longer alone. She turned to see William's soft brown hair and shining eyes in the front row. He smiled and bowed.

"Hail to the Queen!"